REBUILDING HIS DRAGON KINGDOM

BOOK 3 IN THE FIRE AND ICE SERIES

AMELIA SHAW

CHAPTER 1

Cass

    I couldn't believe this was my life now.

Stavrok and Lucy were out tonight, again, negotiating a new trade agreement near the border to the human world. They were always off doing important things. Things that would improve the lives of our people.

And I was left here, holding the babies. *Literally.*

I loved my nephew and his sisters more than anything in the world, but on days like this I longed to be somewhere else. *Anywhere* else.

I clenched my jaw and tightened my hands into fists as I strode along the corridor, a walk I could do with my eyes shut. I knew every inch of this palace back to front. The castle had been my home since I was a little girl. When my parents died, Stavrok had taken me in and raised me like his own.

He'd been young then, barely a year on the throne, and yet he hadn't turned me away when I needed him. He'd always treated me like the little sister he never had. He was part big brother, part father to me.

I was lucky to have him, but lately the walls and ceilings pressed in on me from all sides. I'd begun to feel like a prisoner in my own home. No matter how far I explored, or which paths I took, I always ended up exactly where I started.

That was probably because I wasn't allowed outside the castle walls —had never been, really. Stavrok's rule had only been tighter since that fateful day three years ago when Lucy had been kidnapped and I'd been hurt in the process. Stavrok had really locked things down after that.

I understood why Stavrok kept us close, and safe. But I was turning twenty-one tomorrow, for crying out loud! I was a woman now. My own person, with my own destiny.

I wanted more. I wanted *adventure.* I needed to know what was out there, beyond our green fields and sleepy village.

Most of all, in the heart of my secret desires, I wanted one thing. To go north. To visit the Kingdom of Winter.

Since Stavrok had gone to the north and helped Rage save the North Kingdom, I'd wanted to go myself. See the town that no-one had seen. Meet the people no-one knew about.

I spent most days now, tucked away in the castle library trying to find out more about the mythical town. I read about ice storms and ravenous wolves, harsh winters that lasted for years on end. And huge, powerful dragons that breathed ice instead of fire.

More than anything, I wanted to see everything I read about in the books… for myself.

I walked across the room to a large window and glared out. The view was beautiful, but as familiar as the nose on my face. The snow-peaked mountains, the rolling hills…

An urge struck me: to fling open the windows and let out my dragon. I wanted to stretch my wings and soar. My dragon stirred inside me, and the call for adventure sang through my veins.

I inhaled sharply, pushing away the desire. Then I turned away from the view.

Stavrok forbade me from leaving the castle without an armed guard. As a princess of his realm, I was a valuable hostage; journeying alone was risky. If somebody recognised me, I would make a worthy bride for any upstart warlord or ambitious noble who dared to challenge the king.

I hated being stuck here, no more than a pawn in the games played by the dragon kings.

I wanted to carve my own destiny and while I was Stavrok's cousin, I wasn't sure how I was ever going to do that.

~

In the evening, Stavrok and Lucy returned to the castle.

I smiled with relief when they walked into the dining room, still shaking the last of the snow from their hair. The table was laid with silver candlesticks and the maids had decorated the cloth with sweet floral arrangements. Platters of meat and warm, soft bread were waiting for them.

I stood up from the chair where I rested by the fire and rushed toward them. Lucy greeted me with a hug. She was still cold from being outside, and I shivered in my light evening clothes, pressing my hands to her pink cheeks.

"You're so cold," I said, trying to warm her. As a human, Lucy wasn't as adaptable to our climate as dragon shifters.

"How were my little ones?" Lucy clasped my hands, still shivering as she held my warm palms to her cheeks.

I laughed. "They were good as gold…Well, the girls were!"

Stavrok let out a booming laugh as he took his seat at the head of the table. "My son has a strong will, even now. He will make a fine dragon king one day."

Lucy chuckled and sat beside her husband, reaching out to brush her hand over mine as we all sat down to dinner. "Thanks for watching them, Cass. I know I can always count on you. You're an angel."

I forced out a laugh. "Any time, Lucy."

What else did I have to do?

I fiddled with my fork. "You know I'll always be here."

Always and forever. Until I die of old age, in my library tower, surrounded by my books.

There were worse fates, and yet I couldn't help but want *more*.

Some note of frustration must have come through in my voice, because when I looked up Stavrok had set down the turkey leg he'd been gnawing on and was watching me with a contemplative expression.

I tilted my head. "What's up, cuz?"

A grin slid over his face, and his eyes twinkled. "Cass. Dear Cass."

Uh oh. What have I done now?

"It's your twenty-first birthday tomorrow," Stavrok continued, and my stomach which had lurched at his initial words, relaxed.

A matching grin sparked over Lucy's face, and the two of them turned to me. My heart started to race.

"You're not the child I met anymore, all those years ago." He reached out and took my hand. "You've grown into a beautiful woman. I'm proud of you."

My eyes widened in alarm. "Don't go getting all emotional on me, Stavrok!"

Still, I couldn't help but be a *tiny* bit pleased. If Stavrok thought I was old enough, then that meant…

"I think what my husband is *trying* to say," Lucy interjected, "is that you deserve a treat. A birthday present that will let you… spread your wings, so to speak."

"I'm taking you with me to the north," Stavrok said.

I gasped, both hands going to cover my mouth.

Stavrok grinned, obviously relishing the look of total shock on my face. "To meet the Dragon of Winter himself."

My hands dropped down and my mouth gaped open. The two of them sat there, watching me process the news.

"*Oh. My. God!*" I squealed, launching myself forward to throw my arms around my cousin's neck.

As Stavrok spluttered, struggling to free himself from the embrace, Lucy just sat back and laughed.

Stavrok patted me a few too many times, and I dragged myself back to my seat, barely able to sit still. I was getting out of this king-dom! And they were taking me to the one place I wanted to see!

"I take it this means you're on board with your present?" Lucy said, wiping the tears from her eyes.

"Of *course* I am! I can't believe it!" I relaxed back in my seat. A thousand questions sprang to mind; I didn't know where to begin. "You're being serious, right? You wouldn't trick me with something like this?"

I glanced between my cousin and his wife, both of whom just laughed and shook their heads.

I clapped, too excited to eat. "When do we leave? What do I pack—is it really as cold as they say? Will there be wolves? Will—"

"Whoa!" Stavrok reached out and put a hand on my shoulder, but his eyes were fond. "How about we finish this meal first? Then we can talk about the rest."

"Of course. Thank you, guys! This is seriously..." I couldn't settle on the right word. Eventually, I just went with, "Amazing."

Stavrok and Lucy turned back to their meals. The conversation shifted to the three kids, so I drifted off.

I ate mechanically, without tasting another bite. I wanted to race off to the library at once and bury myself in the old books I had loved since I was little—the tales of the northern explorers, battling against icy storms and fearsome beasts.

I'd never met Damon, the King of Winter, despite the few times he'd come to the castle for royal errands. Stavrok had always kept him, and many of the other kings, away from me for some reason I hadn't yet worked out. I'd only heard stories about Damon, and they were enough to pique my interest to a mountainous level.

The servants passed rumors and I'd gotten snatches of tales traded from person to person, third-or-fourth-hand, from Stavrok's expedi-tions and hunting parties.

Everyone knew that the north was a wild place, ruled by unruly people. Things were different there... survival was harsher. People fought tooth and nail for everything they had.

Their king, according to the rumors, was the wildest one of all. He was said to be a ferocious fighter with piercing eyes and a cold, stoic demeanor. A lifetime spent in the frozen wilderness had rendered him more dragon than man.

An image formed in my mind: a dark, shadowy figure at the center of a snowstorm.

I shivered, and not just from the imagined cold.

My fate was in the north, that much I knew.

The why? That was a mystery.

CHAPTER 2

*C*ass

When I woke the next day—the day we were set to travel —sunlight was already filtering through the curtains and warming my face. I lay there, reveling in the joy and excitement that flooded through me.

It had been so long since I'd traveled, and I didn't even care that Stavrok would be babysitting me the whole time. It was a clear, bright day. I was itching to set out on our journey.

I bounced out of bed, flinging the windows wide open, and inhaled the cool springtime air.

"Someone's ready for their big day," a dry, amused voice said from behind me. "Little Cass, twenty-one years old! You're making me feel my age, child."

I turned around and grinned at Maddie. She was our housekeeper, except she was so much more than that. She was part nanny, part adoptive mother. She'd raised me as much as Stavrok had. Probably more.

She stood in the doorway, hands on her hips. She shook her head at me before moving over to sort out the bedsheets.

I crossed the room and hugged her from behind, making her huff with disapproval at my lack of 'appropriateness'.

"You don't look a day over twenty, Maddie!"

"Flattery will get you nowhere, young lady." Maddie smacked my hands until I backed off, but her eyes were dancing. I was her favorite, and we both knew it. "Now, a little birdie told me about your trip… I take it we've got some packing to do."

I groaned. Packing and choosing clothes was the last thing I wanted to do right now. But Maddie merely tutted at me, opened my huge closet, and ran her hand along the rows of light fabrics.

She began pulling everything out and placing each item on the bed, shaking her head as she went.

It soon became clear that I wasn't exactly prepared for a trip to the far north.

My clothes aren't, anyway.

I was used to the warmth of the castle: if I ventured outside, it was never further than the edge of town. My wardrobe was made up of silk gowns and soft slippers. I found a couple of sweaters tucked at the back, but that was all I had that would save me from freezing to death.

I headed down to the Great Hall, only to find Stavrok there, pacing up and down. Which was odd. He was obviously in a strange mood because, instead of wishing me a happy birthday, he gave me an unreadablelook, like he was agitated about something.

Ugh, forget about him. This is the day everything changes!

"Come this way," Stavrok said, and I let him drag me into the next room.

Lucy and the babies were waiting for me there in the sunroom, along with a luscious birthday breakfast. I shoved aside whatever Stavrok's problem was because I would figure it out later.

Lucy gave me a broad smile.

"I had a surprise for you," she said as she jiggled the toddler on her hip, "but I'm afraid Anselm ate half of it already."

On the low table, a stack of pancakes lay in the centre of a plate, surrounded by strawberries. I squinted at the writing on the top; it was clearly meant to read HAPPY BIRTHDAY CASS, but the top layer had chunks missing. It now read HAP BIR AY CA.

I eyed Anselm with suspicion; he blinked back at me, his eyes wide and innocent.

"I love it!" I smiled, then stuck out my tongue at him while Lucy was distracted by the other two.

He giggled and blew a raspberry back at me.

"Happy birthday, Cass!" Lucy set Anselm down on the floor, then leaned forward to give me a big hug.

Anselm toddled over to where his sisters were stacking wooden bricks. Now that they were all walking, it was impossible to keep them in one place.

"Are you excited?" Lucy asked.

"Finally, a chance to get out of here," I said, trying to sound like I meant it as a joke, but her eyes softened in understanding.

"You deserve it."

I pulled her aside for a moment. "Did something happen this morning?"

She looked puzzled. "Nothing out of the ordinary, why?"

I shook off the uncomfortable feeling, pasting a smile back onto my face. "I'm sure it's nothing."

Ugh, forget about Stavrok!

This was my birthday, and I was going to enjoy every second of it.

"Anything I can help you with?" Lucy asked. "Do you need to borrow a beanie, or muff, or anything?"

"I do, actually! I have nothing suitable for travelling to the north. I'm too used to being here."

Lucy giggled. "And I'm used to being cold all the time! My clothes might be a little big for you, but I'm sure we can get the seamstress to take a few pieces in."

Lucy and I were the same height, but she was much curvier than I was. Especially since giving birth to the triplets.

"Sounds perfect! Thank you so much, Lucy."

Lucy winked at me. "Leave it to me. I'll go have a chat with the seamstress now."

Lucy headed off and I sat on the floor to play with the babies. Only yesterday I was lamenting never being able to leave. And now… I was going to miss them while I was gone.

After breakfast, I went back to my room where three seamstresses came by with a dozen pieces for me to try on. They were all heavy and warm, and I was sweating by the time they were done.

"We'll have these done by the time you leave, Princess," one of the maids said, before she hurried from the room.

"Thank you!" I called out to them, relieved beyond measure that Lucy cared enough to make sure I was comfortable and warm, and still able to go on my dream visit.

By the time we were ready to leave, Stavrok seemed to have gotten over whatever was bothering him earlier. He met me in the hall with the easy smile that dominated his face these days, ever since he'd found Lucy.

"I've sent word to Damon. We will fly to an outpost half a day's journey from the castle, then take the rest on foot."

Huh?

"Why not fly the whole way?" I tilted my head, my confusion only growing when his laughter boomed through the hall.

Several servants turned their heads.

"It would be quicker, right?" I asked him.

"I thought you would prefer to be properly dressed for our arrival, Cassie."

Oh. Right.

Shifters didn't return to human form fully clothed.

I pictured arriving in a strange land, in a strange throne room, naked in front of the fearsome, mysterious King of Winter…

Heat spread across my cheeks.

Stavrok's smile turned fond. "I thought I would spare my favorite cousin the embarrassment."

Favorite… and only cousin!

Irritation prickled over my skin as I realized that he was *protecting* me. I didn't want to be sheltered any more. I wasn't the helpless, vulnerable little girl that everyone around here thought I was.

Still, I couldn't deny the fact I was kind of relieved he'd thought of such a thing. I certainly hadn't.

I didn't want Stavrok to know that, so I just glared and punched him on the arm. It rebounded off his solid frame and he ruffled my hair.

"I've already sent your trunks ahead. The seamstresses worked all night to alter the pieces for you. My men will be waiting for us at a checkpoint just beyond the mountains," he said. "I hope you're ready to stretch your wings."

I grinned. "Absolutely."

We walked through the main hall and stepped onto the balcony. Stavrok stripped off most of his clothes, leaving only his underwear for modesty.

I almost laughed. He only did that for me. Everyone else in the castle had seen him naked a hundred times.

I followed his lead and stripped to my thin chemise and under-wear, lamenting that I was wearing some of my favorite knickers. They'd be shredded soon. I really should have planned that better.

I took my cousin's hand, stepped up onto the balustrade next to him, and took a deep breath as I stared down at the town beneath us. Excitement whipped through my stomach the way the wind was messing with my hair.

"You ready?" Stavrok said.

I nodded.

He jumped, shifting mid-air and swooping low over the town.

I let out a little excited squeal and, letting my shifter take hold of me, threw my human self to the wind.

Taking to the skies again was like a dream.

It had been so long since I'd flown further than the edge of town, and I glided over cloud banks and dipped low over the hilltops, spiraling through the air with the adrenaline singing through my veins.

Stavrok indulged my excitement, but eventually he steered me back on course. I followed him toward the mountains, and together we flew over the smoke-wreathed town in the foothills of the Black Castle.

Rage and Marienne were somewhere below us, tending to their own kingdom. Part of me wanted to stop and say hello, but I was eager to push on.

This was the furthest I'd ever flown from Stavrok's castle. The furthest I'd ever journeyed. *Ever.*

I drank in the colors of the sky, the wind rushing past my wings, the sharp icy chill of the air as we pushed onwards.

Eventually, we started to spiral lower to land. I followed Stavrok until we touched down beside a small cabin in a sparse cluster of trees, and a group of men rushed out to meet us carrying thick robes.

As I shifted, I found myself trembling the instant the cold touched my bare skin. I'd never felt such temperatures before. I wrapped my arms around my bare breasts, my nipples pebbling into hard points from the frost.

And we're not even in the far north yet...

The man who passed me my robe averted his gaze out of respect, though I was sure the men had seen more than they should. I pulled on the robe, hugging the fabric tight around my body and trying not to show my embarrassment. It was hard to hide with my cheeks flushing with heat.

No man had ever seen my naked body, other than in this moment. And when that day finally came, a cold mountainside wasn't exactly the place I had in mind.

Luckily, we were ushered into the cabin before the moment could get too awkward.

Stavrok let out a booming laugh. "Don't worry, Cass." He clapped a heavy hand on my shoulder as he ducked through the doorway. "If any of my men fancy themselves a peek, I'll put their eyes out myself!"

I looked away in horror, only half-sure he was joking. Stavrok could get like that—particularly with Lucy.

I chalked it up to his protective nature, but it was more than that with me. I was a royal dragon shifter, and the men around me sensed the power that came with that title. No one would dare lay a finger on me, but I'd caught their eyes on me more and more often over the past few years as my body had changed into one of a breeding-age woman.

Still chilled to the bone, I scuttled closer to the roaring fire, focusing on warming my face to cover how flustered I was.

"I'm starving," Stavrok said, settling down beside me on the ground and stretching out his legs.

As if on cue, a plate of hot soup and bread was presented to us by one of Stavrok's servants. My stomach lurched and I put my hand to my belly. Damn, I was hungry too. I ate with gusto, tearing into the bread and dipping it into the soup.

"See," Stavrok said, with a note of pride. "You're a little wild thing already!"

I made a face at him but didn't slow down on eating.

When the meal was over, we sat in comfortable silence and stared into the fire's glowing embers.

"I have another surprise for you," Stavrok said. "Lucy and I took a trip to the seamstress last week... She had a hand in the design. Consider it an extra birthday present."

He signaled to the man behind him, and the servant came forward carrying something over his arm. When he held it out for me, I gasped.

"Stavrok!"

Stavrok smiled as I held the garment up in the firelight. It was a long black coat lined with thick gray fur around the collar. The lining was soft and velvety, and when I slipped it on it fit me like a glove. I ran my hands over the delicate patterns stitched into the material, a warmth tingling in my chest.

Something brand new and made just for me. It was such a thoughtful, useful gift.

"It's beautiful." I couldn't help rubbing my cheek over the soft collar. "And so warm!"

"Where we're going, dear one," Stavrok said in a soft voice, "you'll need it."

I was silent, pretending to examine the coat as I mulled over my words. "Stavrok?"

"Yes?"

"What's he like? King Damon?" I bit my lip, regretting my pointed question.

I would never admit it in a thousand years, but a wave of nervous energy flooded through me. I was no stranger to meeting noble families, and powerful men. But this felt… different.

It was my first time visiting his kingdom. I wanted to know what to expect.

What if I make a fool of myself?

Stavrok gave me a strange look. "He inherited a broken kingdom, Cass. A king needs to be extremely strong to overcome such a tragedy."

"But what's he *like?*" I pressed. "Tall? Short? Funny? Boring? I need details, Stavrok."

Stavrok huffed, like I was being unreasonable.

"He's…" He trailed off, staring into the fireplace. "Tall. Are you satisfied, little one?"

"Don't call me that!" I rolled my eyes. "And *don't* avoid the question."

"He's a king like any other," Stavrok said eventually. "We only met once, and we were fighting a battle together. There wasn't much time for small talk, Cass."

I released a long, drawn-out sigh.

There was something he wasn't telling me, but Stavrok wasn't someone I could persuade information out of if he wasn't ready. He'd tell me in his own time.

CHAPTER 3

Cass

Our carriages were waiting for us when we reached past the treeline, with all the belongings we would need for the trip. Given that we didn't know how long that would be, I'd packed practically everything I owned, plus everything Lucy had altered for me before we left.

I grimaced with sympathy at the thought of the servants lugging it all over the mountains.

The men bowed low to Stavrok and me as we stepped up into the carriage.

Once inside, I realized we were on a true royal procession, one royal family visiting another. My heart started to hammer. The anticipation gnawed at me. This was it: the trip I had been waiting for. The journey of a lifetime.

When I looked up, Stavrok was watching me again, a frown on his face.

Annoyance flashed through me.

"What?" I huffed, crossing my arms. "Are you ever going to tell me what's going on?"

He looked down, then stared out of the window at the landscape as we trundled on. I began to wonder if we'd spend the rest of the journey in silence.

"I received word from Queen Marienne."

I brightened up at that. Marienne came to visit Lucy and I whenever she could. She was a natural with the kids, using her magic to make pretty floating lights for them. They loved her as much as we did.

But she had her own kingdom to run, and a new husband, to boot. It had been weeks since I'd heard from her.

"What's wrong?" My heart clenched. "Wait, is she okay?"

"Yes, yes." He waved a hand. "She and Rage are fine... better than fine. She had some news for me, is all."

He paused. The silence weighed heavily between us.

"About you."

I stilled. Marienne's visions were well-known throughout the realm, but this was the first time *my* name had ever been thrown into the mix.

I didn't know what to think.

"What news?" I twisted my hands in my lap. "Did she see something?"

She must have, or Stavrok would never have brought it up.

His mouth pressed together in a thin line. Whatever he was about to tell me, I could see that it troubled him. My stomach tightened beneath my new coat. How bad could the news be?

"She had a vision," he said. "A vision of you. With King Damon. She believes that the two of you are... connected."

He glanced out the window. I could tell he really didn't want to be having this conversation.

I shook my head, totally lost. I couldn't see what the big deal was. We were going to the north to see King Damon, weren't we?

If Marienne saw the future, her vision made sense.

But Stavrok looked *angry*.

"Is *that* what you've been so worked up about?" I snorted. "Some vision of me meeting the king? Hell, I could've predicted that—and I don't have the sight!"

Stavrok twisted around to look at me, his eyes hard. "Cass. You don't understand… Marienne's visions, they don't happen every day. She wouldn't have foreseen this if it wasn't important. She believes that the two of you are fated for one another."

Shock flooded through me.

It can't be true.

"I wanted to cancel this trip," I heard Stavrok say.

I wasn't fully listening anymore, just staring into space, processing the words, hearing them echo in my mind.

Fated for one another.

"But I knew how disappointed you would be. Cass, I'm not saying Marienne is right—"

"Has she ever been wrong?" I asked, my tone sharper than I intended.

Stavrok's face could have been carved from granite. His huge features, usually so warm, were deadly serious. He was more than my cousin. For the first time, I saw him for the man he truly was: a powerful Dragon King.

"All I'm saying is that you need to be prepared."

Prepared for what?

I wanted to call the carriage to a halt. I needed to ask a million questions.

Truth be told, I was terrified. I knew about fated mates—I'd seen it play out right in front of me on the day Stavrok brought Lucy home to the castle.

But it was rare for a dragon shifter to find their perfect match. Like… crazy rare.

I'd never once imagined it might happen to me.

To complicate matters further, I was a virgin. On the occasions I imagined the man I would marry, it was hazy and indistinct, but I'd always pictured something sweet, something romantic. Rose petals and soft music. *Definitely* not the crazed, lust-fueled pursuit that came to mind when I pictured a mate's heat.

Something must have shown on my face, because Stavrok leaned forward until I looked up to meet his gaze.

"Cass, listen to me. I won't let anything happen to you. I swear." He straightened up, his bulk spanning almost the width of the carriage. "I'm here as your guardian. I'll protect you—like I always have."

Outside, the landscape was changing. The trees were gone; the landscape consisted of miles of frozen ground, as far as the eye could see. Inside the carriage was warm, but I shivered all the same.

"How much further?" I mumbled.

I forced the whole conversation out of my mind. I had come here to explore, to see the world, and I was going to do that no matter what.

Stavrok pointed at a distant tower poking over the horizon out of the carriage window. "We're almost there."

As the carriage wheels turned and the horses picked up the pace, I barely heard the small talk from Stavrok. I couldn't hear anything beyond the rushing in my ears, and my own thudding heart. It completely drowned out everything else.

Why did it feel like I was about to meet my destiny head-on?

It was mid-afternoon by the time we arrived at the castle gates. The sky was pale gray, and snow blustered in through the door when Stavrok opened it. A blast of cold air hit me, and I turned up the collar of my coat as I stepped outside.

My eyes widened as I took in the huge castle with its ancient drawbridge. A wide moat surrounded the fortress; laid out around it was what looked like a giant building site.

"King Damon's enemies razed the whole town to the ground," Stavrok said as we walked along a winding, makeshift path. Everywhere I looked, townsfolk were hard at work, bricklaying, sawing, and heaving huge blocks of stone over the frozen ground. "They've been slow to rebuild. The conditions up here can be brutal."

I craned my neck to watch the drawbridge as it lowered to let us over the moat. Everywhere I looked there were remnants of the battle, deep gouges in the stonework and burn marks over the battlements that could have only been done by dragon fire.

"It's so…" I trailed off, lost for words at the huge, imposing structure.

All the castles I had seen were square and smooth, made of sandstone. This castle was all dizzying turrets and spiky towers, edged with snowdrifts.

"So tall," I said eventually, letting out a nervous laugh.

Stavrok grinned, leading me up to the huge front doors. The guardsmen stepped aside, bowing low, to let us pass.

Back home, the palace guards were friendly and open with me. I knew all their names; after all, most of them had watched me grow up.

These guards were different. They were fearsome in their thick overcoats, and the broadswords by their sides looked like they had seen their fair share of use.

The hallway was as grand and stately as I expected, and even Stavrok looked impressed. He glanced up at a huge window as we passed underneath an elaborate stone archway, whistling.

"The last time I was here, this room was nothing but rubble," he said, catching my eye. "I hardly even recognize the place."

As Stavrok continued to admire the repair work, I trailed after him. I tried to keep up, but in truth I was barely paying attention to the running commentary.

Now that we were in the castle, it was impossible to forget about Marienne's vision. The man I was about to meet could very well be my intended mate. The one person who was designed for me, and me for him.

Part of me wanted to run screaming from the place. The other part was so excited I could barely walk straight. I'd wanted a life, and an adventure, outside the safety of Stavrok's castle, and I'd gotten it. In spades.

We were led deeper and deeper down the cavernous hallways. Our guide, another stone-faced guard, made me nervous. I stuck close to Stavrok's side, my mind racing.

My palms itched with anticipation. I tried to imagine this king, a total stranger, somewhere in the castle. Could he feel my presence?

What if what Marienne had foretold was true?

I swallowed as Stavrok indicated I should move forward, and together we walked into a small antechamber. Two more guards waited on either side of a huge door. They stared at us impassively as we approached and knocked once on the huge double doors.

My heart stalled in my chest. It was too late to turn back now.

DAMON

"Sire." The voice of my chief advisor startled me out of my thoughts. "They're here."

I straightened and stood up from my throne, striding forward into the center of the room. It was customary to greet a fellow king on equal ground. I could not meet my guests from high on my throne.

The formal clothes I wore were stiff and uncomfortable. I much preferred to wear my everyday attire, but my advisors had cautioned against it. I found all the court rules and regulations stifling, especially when my mind and my focus was on the repair work I'd been carrying out with my men this morning.

Still. Stravrok had shown me great generosity during the battle by coming to our aid. Not to mention what he'd done for us since we started repairing. It was only fitting that I return that favor by allowing him and his cousin to visit and see the renovations.

Plus, it gave me a chance to show the other kingdoms that we were slowly regaining our former strength. My ancient house—the family of ice dragons that had ruled the north for generations—had survived the raiders.

The castle wasn't the only thing my father had driven to ruin. I needed to rebuild alliances and treaties. The best way to do that was to make peace with my fellow rulers.

The corners of my mouth lifted into a polite, welcoming smile as the doors opened.

"His Majesty, King Stavrok of the Bravdok Clan, and his cousin, the Princess Cassandra."

Stavrok strode into the room with all the brazen confidence I remembered. The years since the battle hadn't changed him that much; only a few more threads of silver in his hair indicated that time had passed.

I greeted him with a nod, and he grinned back, charging over with his hand outstretched, ready to pull me into a friendly bear hug.

He only managed to get halfway to me, however, before I caught sight of the other newcomer standing behind him.

My dragon woke from its slumber, uncoiling inside my chest. I gasped, trying to push him down.

Something I'd never felt before pulsed through my veins, dark and hot, filling me with a single-minded purpose: a *desire* like I'd never known before.

What the hell is this?

Whatever it was, I had no power to stop it.

My vision began to change. Everything in the room faded out of focus. And nothing else mattered. Not my kingdom. Not my castle repairs. Not the fact that I was a king.

Only *she* remained.

Her chestnut brown hair hung in loose curls, dusted with snowflakes from her journey. Her eyes were wide and fringed with dark lashes. Unlike most of the shifters I had met, who all had icy, pale blue eyes, hers were a deep, warm brown.

I need her.

The realization hit me like an anvil. I didn't know what it meant. And I didn't have time to work it out. I strode forward, my gaze zeroed in on my prize.

Stavrok stepped in front of her, blocking my path. He knocked away my hands outstretched for her. I let out a deep growl, prepared to shift if I needed to fight the other man. My neighboring king.

Stavrok was on the brink of fighting as well. I caught sight of his dragon when his angry gaze flashed to meet mine. Hot rage curled within me and I lowered my stance. Stavrok would not keep her from me.

She wasn't any woman. This one was mine.

I knew the difference. I'd had women before. I was a Dragon King, and I had to satisfy my appetite for pleasure alongside everything else.

The stresses of recent years meant I'd tamped down my desire. In the face of all I had to build, a fumble with a maid or some woman in town felt like a waste of time. I had responsibilities, more important things to deal with than my sex drive.

Not that women hadn't put themselves in my path. I was their king. More often than not, I'd rebuffed them.

And this was why. *She* was why.

All thought of polite pleasantries and formal introductions were long gone. Stavrok and I circled each other, Stavrok keeping himself between me and the girl as I snarled with impatience.

We weren't two kings anymore, ready for an official royal visit. This was deeper. Primal.

We were dragon shifters and the need to fight this invader, this intruder in my kingdom, coursed through me as strong as the ocean.

For whatever reason, the mere sight of this girl inflamed my dragon like no other.

Only one thing remained: the feral, frenzied, uncontrollable urge to take her and carry her out of here.

Stavrok shouted something, but I was too far gone to hear it. I could only watch, burning with fury, as he grabbed the girl by the arm and practically dragged her out of the room.

The moment the heavy door thudded closed behind them, I was at the door, pounding against the wood. My shifter writhed in frustration; it was all I could do not to release my anger, shift, and burn down my own door to get to her.

"Stavrok!" I heard myself bellow, fists balled against the immovable oak door. "Open the door, right now!"

"So, it is true," the voice came back, muffled, from the other side of the door. "Marienne was right."

I was losing patience. As every minute passed, shifting looked like a more and more appealing plan.

"What is true?"

"You're my cousin's true match. Her fated mate," Stavrok yelled through the door.

I forced myself to take deep, ragged breaths, fighting to regain control. It was easier now that the girl wasn't in the same room, but knowing exactly where she was, just out of reach… the feeling of it, the knowledge… It was pure torture. I groaned.

"The two of you are destined for each other."

I pressed my forehead against the door, growling. "Then what are you waiting for? Let me through!"

"You're not in control, Damon!"

I bared my teeth at him, unseen. Frustration pounded through me.

"She's young…" Stavrok hissed. "And still a virgin!"

"Stavrok!" Another voice cut in. A sweet, light voice, admonishing him for revealing a truth that had my dragon retreating slowly.

I straightened when I heard her voice, crowding as close as possible up against the door and hoping she would speak again.

"Get yourself together," Stavrok said. "I'm warning you. If you can't control your dragon, I will leave, and I'll take Cass with me. You'll never see her again."

He sounded dangerous; deadly. If I were in my right mind, I would have been afraid. Stavrok was a fearsome warrior. I had no doubt that if anything happened to his beloved cousin, he would have my head for it.

I focused on breathing, clearing the fog that had spread through my senses.

"Okay." I took a few steps back from the door. "I'm ready."

*D*amon

Slowly, the doors opened.

Stavrok stood with his arms crossed, half in front of Cassandra. She sidled out from around him.

I worried that my behavior had terrified her. One glance told me otherwise, from the lust burning in her gaze, to the way a light flush had spread over her cheeks.

I forced down a shiver and turned my attention back to Stavrok.

"My apologies," I said through gritted teeth. "Your cousin caught me by surprise."

Stavrok's face was stony, and I could tell he was holding back on me for Cass's sake. He nodded, straightening up, posturing and protective.

My dragon simmered with rage at the show of strength. I knew better than to challenge him, because when it came to the safety of his cousin, Stavrok was indeed doing the right thing. Even if my dragon couldn't see it yet.

You could have cut the tension in the room with a blade. One wrong move, and the peace I'd built—this fragile alliance I wanted to strengthen between my kingdom and the others—could be reduced to ashes.

We stood in silence, my head buzzing.

"Well," Stavrok said loudly, clapping his hands together. "Do we get the grand tour?"

"Of course," I replied, grateful for the suggestion. "Follow me…"

I LED THEM THROUGH THE CASTLE, FOCUSING MY MIND ON ANYTHING but the woman walking with Stavrok. I pointed out all the changes I'd made and moved as if in a trance. The voices around me were muffled, like I was underwater.

After a while, Stavrok stepped out in front and led the way, talking loudly and asking question after question. He seemed keen to put as much space between me and his cousin as possible.

Cass herself was an enigma.

I could barely keep my eyes off her. She flitted through the hallways, her gaze wide and excited at every detail, every new discovery. Occasionally she stole a glance at me, and I looked away the moment our eyes met, glaring at the floor.

I didn't trust my dragon not to grab her if he had half the chance.

Her long dark hair tumbled around her shoulders in loose curls, and her eyes were warm and bright. Everything about her was a breath of fresh air in this cold, gloomy place. She reminded me of a butterfly in the way she darted from window to window.

My dragon ached for her. More than anything, I wanted to grab her and haul her away somewhere, *anywhere* we could be alone. Then I could unleash all my passion and drive her into ecstasy.

But a small part of me—the tiny shred of reason buried in the back of my mind—told me that Stavrok was right about not rushing this connection I was feeling with Cass.

I couldn't risk offending Stavrok. And I couldn't risk her safety.

Outside, the snowflakes tumbled thicker and faster as we reached the rear of the castle, where the high walls overlooked the small gardens below.

Cass tapped on the windows. "What's that down there?"

"The hedge maze," I said.

Her eyes lit up with curiosity at the prospect of an adventure.

"My ancestors planted it centuries ago."

Stavrok's eyes narrowed. "Cass, you're not going out there in this. It's going to be a blizzard before long."

Cass tilted her chin up at him defiantly. "It's my birthday, isn't it? We didn't come all this way so I could end up stuck inside another castle… No offence," she added, glancing at me.

Heat gathered in my chest as her eyelashes swept across her cheek.

"None taken," I murmured, pretending intense interest in the weather beyond the window as Stavrok and Cass debated behind me.

Eventually, Cass won the argument and as I turned to look at them, Stavrok frowned at me.

I wasn't the ally he hoped for. In this state, I was hardly going to deny her request. My dragon wanted to give Cass everything.

I'll protect her.

As we headed down to the small gatehouse at the foot of the castle, emerging into the frosty air on the long, winding path that took us toward the gardens, Cass appeared suddenly, bobbing up beside my elbow.

I shuddered with longing as she brushed against my arm. The pink that rose in her cheeks had nothing to do with the cold air.

"What's in the middle?" she asked.

I turned to look at her, my eyes trailing downward. She was a petite little thing, only coming up to my shoulder. I didn't trust myself to speak, so I waited for her to clarify.

"Of the maze," she added, then bit her lip.

I groaned internally, imagining what it would be like to sink my teeth into her soft flesh.

"Don't mazes usually have a prize in the middle?"

Her gaze lingered over mine. I couldn't help but wonder what kind of *prize* she was imagining.

There were plenty of places for two people to get lost inside a maze.

Perhaps that's what she's counting on?

Stavrok was glowering by the time we reached the entrance of the maze. The tall hedges on either side were already covered in a fine bank of snow. A glance up to the sky didn't tell me much. The weather could turn, or it could hold.

Behind Stavrok, Cass was admiring a frost-tipped rose. The color matched her glowing cheeks. She was utterly bewitching.

I would give her anything she wanted.

The knowledge terrified me. I glowered, hoping that my fascination didn't show on my face.

"Are you sure you want to do this?" Stavrok grumbled, flicking snow off the edge of his coat.

Cass grinned up at him. He sighed, mumbling something about birthdays and annoying cousins, but followed her into the maze without a backward glance.

I trailed after them. My dragon was still simmering inside me, barely contained; the urge to grab her thudded continuously in the back of my mind. If anything, it was growing stronger with each twist and turn of the maze. Cass led us deeper and deeper. Stavrok swore when he stumbled over an exposed tree root, grumbling to himself.

The hedges closed around us.

Cass practically ran around each bend in the hedgerows. It turned into a game of chase. My heart raced as I tracked her through the maze. My dragon was single-minded and greedy; it wanted her.

She skipped ahead, throwing a cheeky smile back at me. I caught the edge of a skirt, a loose curl, before she slipped out of sight around the corner.

I glanced behind me. Stavrok was nowhere to be seen.

I was alone.

There was nothing for it but to go on. The sky above was white with snowflakes, which were falling thicker and faster than ever.

"Cass?" I shouted. "Stavrok?"

I listened intently but there was no answer, only the wind rustling through the leaves around me.

I knew the maze better than most. When I was a child, I often played in it, or hid away where the servants couldn't find me when my father was on one of his rampages. But as I got closer to the middle, my worry grew. I could make it out of here, but Cass and Stavrok…

Get to Cass, my dragon growled. *Find her. Protect her. Take her.*

I rounded the corner and got my bearings, realizing I was close to the center. My heart rate picked up when I heard a voice behind me, high and sweet.

"King Damon?"

I turned. Cass stood in the middle of the path. She had her arms wrapped around her body, tucked into herself, and she was trembling as gust after gust of cold air buffeted the hedgerows around her and sent her hair tumbling and flying within a cascade of snowflakes.

"This way," I said, unwilling to get too near her.

I strode down the path, leading the way. Her footsteps trotted as she caught up with me.

"We need to get out of here!" Her voice trembled.

The snowstorm was building, and it wouldn't be long before we were trapped in it.

"Shouldn't we turn around?"

She was right. We needed to get under cover, and fast.

There wasn't time to get back to the castle. I swallowed thickly as I realized that we only had one option.

"You wanted to know what was at the center of the maze." I strode onwards. The path narrowed, and I knew what waited for us around the next corner. "Didn't you?"

"Well, yes, but…"

I turned and stared at her. "Trust me."

Our eyes met. Heat sparked through my veins. Her breathing grew ragged. The fur on her collar rose and fell with each exhale.

She nodded.

Together, we turned the final corner.

We had reached the center of the maze. Alone.

In the middle of the clearing stood the entrance to the stone grotto that led to the caves.

I ushered Cass toward the entrance. The snow was falling so thickly that I could barely make out the stony entrance. As Cass hurried to the grotto, I ducked outside to take a final look around for Stavrok.

He was nowhere to be seen.

Cursing the weather, I ran into the cave.

"Cass!" My voice echoed off the rocky walls. I climbed down the steps cut into the rock.

Her soft footsteps shuffled up ahead. My heart pounded with adrenaline. We were alone.

I should never have agreed to show them the gardens. I knew the weather would get worse.

They aren't from around here. They don't know how harsh our winters are. They're used to rolling hills and mild snowdrifts.

I could only blame my misjudgment on my foggy head and the overpowering lust that I couldn't shake. It was more potent than anything I'd felt before, and my body wouldn't let me forget that the source of my misery was a scant two feet away from me.

"Damon?" Cass called again, nearer this time.

I stepped into the cavern. Dim light flickered from a torch set into the stone wall, casting a golden glow over the stone. Cass had her back to me, staring into the pool that dominated the room, watching the steam rise from it and spiral upwards.

"It's a hot spring," I heard myself say, coming over to stand beside her. From this close I could feel the warmth from her body. "People swim here sometimes. It's said that the water has healing properties."

She glanced up at me. "Can I...?"

Once I realized what she was asking, I stiffened.

We would be stuck here for some time, until the storm lifted. She was cold and wanted to go in, and with her staring at me like that I couldn't think of a good reason why not.

The second I nodded, she began to unbutton her coat, sliding the fabric down and off her shoulders.

A growl rose unbidden to my lips. I turned my back on her and strode over to the other side of the cave, toward the mouth of the tunnel.

"Where are you going?"

Her voice was light, teasing. She was taunting me.

"Nowhere," I forced myself to say as I stared down at a wooden chest by the entrance to the cave. It had clean clothes and towels, if I remembered correctly, but couldn't make myself reach down to open the lid. My body was wound far too tightly.

A soft rustle reached my ears, the sound of fabric dropping to the floor. I clenched my hands into fists when the gentle sounds of lapping water reached me. Then I heard her body slide beneath the surface.

I swallowed, squeezing my eyes closed.

"It's warm!" Her tone was startled, as though she couldn't believe that up here in the freezing mountains, beneath the arid earth, were warm springs.

But I heard the sweet undercurrent of pleasure in her words and began to imagine how she'd look swimming through the water.

I forced myself to relax and draw deep, even breaths.

The mere thought of her naked body sliding beneath the water was maddening. I could hear the gentle splash as she moved around, but I didn't dare look.

"Aren't you joining me, my king?" Her tone was teasing, and her words even more so.

That was the last straw.

I rounded on her. "What game are you playing at?"

She stood in the middle of the pool. She was submerged up to her bare shoulders. Curly tendrils of her dark hair lay on the water's surface. She looked like a nymph.

Or a siren. Come to lead me to my doom.

"What do you mean?"

She sounded shocked. Her eyes, however, raked up and down my body. I had only deigned to remove my outer coat, and I stood before her in my shirt and slacks. Strangely, I felt like I was the naked one.

"You want me to swim with you? Alone, in this cave? With..." I gritted my teeth, waving a hand to indicate her bare form. "Your cousin—"

"My cousin," Cass interrupted, her eyes flashing with impatience, "is not here."

CHAPTER 5

*D*amon

Cass stilled, and then looked up at me again. There was a new fire in her eyes, burning even brighter than before.

I hadn't realized that she must have been kneeling until she stood up in the pool and revealed herself to me. Droplets of water rolled down the contours of her body, hugging her curvaceous frame. My eyes raked over every inch of her hips, her pale thighs, her small high breasts.

She was still, silent. It was a challenge.

She had thrown down the gauntlet, baring herself to me.

My dragon ignited inside me, recognizing its mate once again. I let out an inhuman growl and crashed into the water, still clothed. Cass squealed with surprise as I wrapped my arms around her waist and hoisted her body flush against mine.

We both groaned at the feel of finally being able to touch each other. Her legs tightened around my waist. I backed her through the water until I reached the place where the rock leveled out, creating a natural shelf in the side of the cave. I pressed her against it, and she arched her back, revealing her long, pale throat to me.

It was an act of submission in the boldest possible way.

She wants this. Wants me to claim her.

The dragon was in control now. My teeth scraped against the sensitive flesh, and she whimpered, her hands running along my forearms as she bucked and writhed against me. I gripped her hips, holding her in place, while she pulled my shirt out, tracing over the planes of my chest.

I drew back, breathing harshly. Her lips were red and full where she'd bitten into them, and her eyes were hazy, pupils blown out with desire. I was willing to bet I didn't look much saner.

My fingers slid up her thighs and she squirmed with delight. Knowing I was the first man to touch her in such a way was intoxicating.

My dragon pushed for more, *more*, and I gave into it fully.

I grunted when her hand closed around the nape of my neck, tugging my hair with impatience. Her eyes flashed, and I knew her own dragon guided every movement, from the way her hips bucked up into mine to her other hand clinging against my back, pushing up my shirt, greedy for more contact.

When my hands slid between her thighs and my fingers pushed inside her wet pussy, we both gasped. Her hot, open mouth pressed against my shoulder, and I groaned at the feel of her sharp teeth against my skin, and how tight she was around me.

She clung to me, wet hair sticking to my shoulders as we moved together. My thumb circled her clit and she tensed, tightening even further.

When she reached for my cock, I growled, grabbing both of her hands in one of mine and pinning them above her head, to the cave wall behind her. My own pleasure could wait.

She acquiesced to the restriction, staring up at me with wide, lust-filled eyes.

I teased her, withdrawing my fingers so that I could run my free hand over her breasts, cupping them as I bruised her throat with kisses before returning to her pussy. Even submerged in water, I could feel how hot and wet she was inside, and it drove me wild.

When she squeezed tight around my fingers, a long moan sounding in my ear, I couldn't hold back my dragon any longer.

When I pulled my fingers out, she whimpered at the loss of contact. Her hands fumbled for me, and together we pushed down my trousers so that there was nothing standing between us.

I lined up my cock with her still-squirming body and thrust into her as slowly as I could considering the lust riding me hard. She cried out in shock and pleasure, wrapping her arms and legs around me tight, holding me close.

Around us the surface of the water trembled, and the torch flames fluttered. The force of our shifters joining together filled the cave with an energy I'd never seen before, a light that drove the shadows away and illuminated the pool. I could feel the power flowing through my body, and from the look on Cass's face, I could tell that she did, too.

I thrust into her over and over again, feeling her squeeze tighter and tighter around my cock with every forward motion of my hips. Nothing had ever felt so right, so perfect. Every cry, every moan, every gasp from her lips was like a symphony to my ears.

Then her small frame began to stiffen against me, and her sharp cry filled the cave as her orgasm overtook her. She rode it out against me, and after a couple of harsh thrusts I followed her over the edge.

For several endless moments I stood there in the water, braced against her.

We were both panting and the water around us suddenly felt cold against my overheated skin. I pulled out, stroking a shaking hand down her side before I could stop myself. I tucked my cock away and staggered out of the water.

Guilt hammered me, choking the life out of the afterglow that flowed through me. I was sated, satisfied, and utterly screwed.

This beautiful, innocent girl… I'd taken her. Without a second thought. My dragon had overruled my better judgment and I'd done the one thing I swore I would not do until my kingdom was repaired: I had claimed my mate.

My kingdom still lay in ruins around me. I spent all my days, and many of my nights, rebuilding the castle and the land surrounding it, shoring up our defences in preparation for winter. My world was one of ice and fire. The land was harsh and hostile, and only harsh things grew on it.

The people were tough. They had to be, in order to weather anything that the north threw at them. Cass was slender, beautiful, and delicate. She was a hothouse flower, a rare creature in a such a cold climate.

Such beauty surely couldn't survive the ice.

I swallowed as she climbed out of the water behind me.

After everything was said and done, I was no better than my father. The man had terrorized this country for so long. He'd been selfish and weak. He'd taken without a second thought.

And now I'd done exactly the same.

"Damon?"

I half turned my head. Mercifully, she'd slipped on her dress. It clung to her damp body, and I looked away before my baser instincts could wreck further havoc.

"The snow should have eased off by now," I said. "We need to return to the castle before nightfall."

"Okay."

She sounded so despondent that I turned to look at her properly. A stab of remorse ran through me when I realized she was shivering.

I strode over to the wooden chest near the entrance to the cave, rifling through it until I found a towel.

"Here." I returned to her, draping the towel around the exposed skin of her shoulders and wrapping it firmly around her. "Use this."

She gave me a wan smile, and I picked up her coat, helping her into it.

"What about you?" Her eyes flicked over my soaking form, and I remembered abruptly that I was still fully clothed.

At the sight of her naked body, all common sense had gone out the window. I couldn't help the sheepish smile that crept over my face.

I played it off, shrugging. "I'm from the north. We're cold-blooded up here."

Her eyes glimmered, and the corners of her mouth twitched. "Is that so? Well, you could've fooled me."

She glanced at the hot pool behind her, as if to remind me wordlessly of our heated encounter.

Like I needed reminding. My face remained stoic, but my heart was still beating a mile a minute in my chest. I regretted the loss of control, whatever my body told me. Whatever the dragon inside me wanted.

Who am I kidding? If my dragon had its way, we'd already be going for round two.

"Come on," I said, changing the subject. "Your cousin is probably worried sick."

Without waiting for a response, I picked up my own coat from where it lay in a crumpled heap on the floor and pulled it on. Then, I strode toward the mouth of the cave.

I needed to put some space between us. That was all I needed. Time to think, to clear my head.

The cold air hit me and my wet clothes hard, but the snow had thankfully eased off.

The sooner we were out of this maze, the better.

CHAPTER 6

*C*ass

The journey back up to the castle, despite my best attempts at conversation, was mostly silent.

Damon didn't hesitate in getting out of the maze. He probably had the route memorized. With his longer legs, I almost had to jog to keep pace with him, but I didn't mind. It helped take my mind off the cold.

Occasionally I felt his eyes on me, but he always dropped his gaze before I could get a read on him. There was worry in his expression though, and his broad shoulders were stiff with tension.

It didn't make sense. Back in the cave, he'd been passionate and intense. Everything I'd ever dreamed a lover would be.

Things had been simple between us there. I wanted him, and he wanted me.

Now he was evasive.

I tried to make the best of the heavy silence and use the time to organize my thoughts. Everything had happened so fast. The last few hours were a jumbled-up blur of sensations. It was hard not to let the excitement of the day overwhelm me. I felt like a totally different person to the girl who had woken up that morning.

From the second I'd laid eyes on Damon, my dragon had

responded, hungry for his touch. We'd gone from room to room, down every hallway and explored every inch of his castle. Nothing slaked the burning fire in my belly.

I'd thought the fresh air might help matters, but I had no such luck. I had been aching for him to take me; my only thought had been to lure him deeper, somewhere away from prying eyes.

I thought we'd both gotten what we wanted.

I guess I was wrong.

The second we were inside the castle, he muttered something about needing a change of clothes and hurried into another room. The door slammed shut behind him with a resounding *thud.*

I lingered in the hallway. My hair was still dripping with melted snow and water from the heated spring pool. The soft sound of water dripping against the tiles on the floor was the only noise in the empty space.

The ecstasy from the cave felt like a far-off dream. I'd woken up to the cold, harsh light of day, and my happiness gave way to doubt.

What does this mean? What will happen if he doesn't want me?

Ice filled the pit of my stomach.

I wasn't sure how I long I stood there, turning every detail over in my mind. Now that the initial frenzy of lust had been satisfied, I could look at things more objectively.

Did I do something wrong?

I thought back to the way Damon held me against him, his firm hands on my hips, his hot mouth on my neck. The way he thrust into me, claiming me…

I bit my lip, the heat rising in my cheeks once again as lust twisted in my belly, making me ache for more.

He *had* wanted me, that much had been clear.

So why can he barely look at me now?

"Cass?"

I turned, relief flooding me at the familiar voice. I'd never been so happy to see my cousin.

"Stavrok!" I rushed over to him. "We lost you back there. Are you all right?"

Stavrok's eyes flickered on the word *we* but he otherwise ignored my phrasing.

He grunted, looking unhappy. "The way back to the castle was easy enough from the air," he said. "I shifted as soon as the weather turned. I looked for you, Cass, but I couldn't see you. I thought you must have returned to the castle, but…"

He tilted his head. I could see the cogs turning in his mind, and I fiddled with my fingers, twisting them around each other, uncomfortable.

"Damon found me." My eyes flicked over to a nearby tapestry.

Stavrok's gaze burned a hole in the side of my face, but I ignored him.

"There were these underground caves, and…"

I trailed off. My cheeks grew hot. I reached up and pressed a hand against one, trying to hide my face behind my hair.

"I see," Stavrok said.

After his earlier attitude, I expected him to explode with anger. In the back of my mind, I feared he would tear apart the castle, kill Damon, and carry me home with him.

But he didn't sound enraged. Instead, he seemed…resigned.

I looked up. "You're not mad at me?"

His gaze softened as he looked down at me. "Cass, I could never be mad at you."

"We just…" I scrambled for a response. A thousand excuses for my behavior fell into my head: the weather, the cave, the water. The way Damon looked at me, how good his hands had felt…

Stavrok *definitely* wouldn't appreciate hearing all the details.

But I had to make him *understand.*

"It just happened," I whispered. "It's like Marienne said. Like you said. I think it was always going to happen."

Stavrok huffed, but he nodded. His hands rested on my shoulders, and we stood together in the quiet.

"When I look at you, I still see that tiny girl who showed up at the castle gates one night with nowhere else to go." In a familiar, comforting gesture, Stavrok tugged gently on a lock of my hair.

"You've always been a sister to me, Cass. It's hard for me to admit that you've grown up."

"I know."

He gave a heavy sigh and stepped backwards. "It seems that I owe Marienne once again."

We smiled at each other.

Then, Stavrok's face grew serious. "Cass, it's probably best if I head home. I only came to introduce you to Damon, and to protect you from his dragon if it was needed. But you've proven you can handle him well enough on your own, and well… I need to return. I have my own kingdom to run."

A shiver of loss ran through me.

All this time, Stavrok had been a necessary endurance. My chaperone, an annoying brother figure standing in the way of my destiny.

The thought of him going, left me cold. He was the one constant in this place, my only reminder of home.

He gave me a regretful smile. "You don't need me here, Cass."

"I *know*, but—"

I bit my lip to stop myself from continuing. I sounded petulant.

The truth was, I was afraid, alone in a frozen fortress with a mate who was a stranger to me.

"That's only if you want to stay?" Stavrok asked, lifting an eyebrow. "Or have I read you wrong? You can come home with me also, if you'd like?"

The idea of leaving now filled me with an even greater dread. Damon was my destiny, my fate. I was sure of it. I couldn't leave him now.

I looked straight at my cousin and smiled as confidently as I could. "I want to stay."

Stavrok nodded. "I knew you would. I'm so proud of the woman you've become, Cass. I know you'll do *me* proud and if you have any issues with the Winter King, you know you can always come home."

I grinned at him. "In this weather?"

He shrugged. "You're a royal, Cass. Shift and fly home. We'll be there waiting with open arms, no matter what."

Tears filled my eyes as I embraced my cousin, my protector, my king. "Thank you Stavrok."

He was right.

I was a grown woman now.

If I wanted a life of my own, I'd have to take it.

Stavrok had taken his leave and night had fallen in the castle. Damon did not reappear.

The servants showed me up the winding staircase to a cozy suite of rooms. I huddled gratefully beside the roaring fireplace, watching the snow drift past the windows. The fur throws strewn over the bed were thick and soft to the touch, and I tugged one over my shoulders while I stared into the flames.

He was avoiding me.

I called out for a maidservant. It was a matter of minutes before the door opened, and a woman entered. She was a slip of a thing, scarcely older than I was, and she eyed me with poorly disguised nerves.

"Can I help you, Your Highness?"

"King Damon." I stood, letting the fur blanket slide onto my chair. "Where is he?"

The maid looked even more nervous at my question. I softened my expression, hearing Stavrok's words echo around my head.

You're a stranger to them, remember? They're not used to outsiders. You'll have to win over their trust, little by little.

"I… I'm not sure, ma'am."

We stared at each other.

We both knew she was lying.

In all likelihood, he slept in another part of the castle altogether. He had tucked me away in one of the guest bedrooms.

Out of sight, out of mind.

"Very well," I said eventually, defeated. For now.

The maid bobbed a curtsy before she turned to leave. A thought struck me, and I put up a hand.

"Wait."

She turned back, her eyebrows drawing together with confusion. "Can I help you with anything else, Your Highness?"

I bit my lip. "I only wanted to ask… your name."

"My name?" She sounded surprised. "It's Isla, ma'am."

"Isla." I repeated the unfamiliar name, giving her a genuine smile. "Thank you for your help, Isla."

With one final, curious glance at me, the maid was gone.

I thought longingly of my maids at home. Of Maddie. She scolded me constantly over reading too much, leaving my clothes in a mess and failing to follow the formal etiquette of the royal houses—among other things—and she didn't suffer fools lightly.

I wrapped myself in the blanket and burrowed down into its warmth, staring into the flames. I would give anything to see Maddie again, even if I would most likely get a lecture on disappearing into hedge mazes with strange men…

Hell, I even miss the babies.

I returned to staring at the flames.

Coming here had turned my world upside down. Nothing was what I expected. I'd flown farther than I ever had before, lost my virginity, and found the man that Marienne claimed was my fated mate.

A fated mate who can barely look at me. And I have no idea why.

I gave myself a mental shake.

Dammit. I was the Princess Cassandra of the Kingdom of Bravdok, cousin to King Stavrok. I was a dragon shifter, and a powerful one at that.

Nothing was going to dampen my spirits.

I *wanted* to be here. No matter how nervous I was, how alone I felt now that Stavrok was gone…

Maybe winning over Damon was impossible. I could be fighting a losing battle, wanting love from a man who had none to give.

Something told me not to give up hope. I'd wanted adventure, hadn't I? Well, now I had it.

I stared at the carved wolves over the fireplace. In the flickering orange glow of firelight, they almost seemed alive, twisting and fighting with each other along the wooden panel. The broad reindeer antlers hanging over the fire cast long shadows against the back wall.

Maybe I could belong here.

The question was though, how could I get Damon to see it?

CHAPTER 7

C *ass*

I woke the next day bright and early, my mind made up.

I sat bolt upright, smiling broadly to myself like a mad woman. I had a plan.

Damon could be as stoic and silent as he wanted.

I wasn't going to let it get to me. I would enjoy myself, just as I'd intended to before all this business of soul mates, and the irresistible desire that came with it, got in the way.

He can like it or lump it. I don't care.

I flung off the covers and toed on the fur-lined slippers that lay waiting for me by the fireplace. A glance out of the window told me that the snowfall was lighter today. *Yes*! I would get a chance to see the countryside I'd been aching to explore for years. My stomach tightened with anticipation as I thought about the day that lay ahead.

A sharp knock at the door startled me.

"Come in!" I called out as I bounced over to the huge wardrobe. All my clothes were hung up neatly inside, waiting for me.

"Your Highness." The door creaked open, and I smiled over my shoulder in the general direction of Isla's voice. "I came to ask if you'd like for me to bring you some breakfast."

I waved her off.

"I'll eat with Damon," I said happily, then did a double take as her eyes widened. "What's wrong?"

"The king… usually doesn't like to be disturbed, ma'am. He takes his meals in his study."

I wrinkled my nose. "Well, let's surprise him."

Isla looked frightened by this prospect, but I breezed over it. I had other things to think about.

I grabbed her elbow and steered her toward the open wardrobe. "Can you help me pick out some clothes?"

"Um." Isla glanced at the rows of garments, then back at me, seemingly at a total loss. "I suppose… yes?"

I grinned with triumph. Rifling through my dresses, I pulled out a simple blouse with a lacy, open neck. "This is one of my favorites. What do you think?"

"I think you'll freeze before you take a step outside," Isla muttered, before slapping a hand over her mouth. "I intended no disrespect, Your Highness. I only meant…"

I snorted and pushed the offending garment back into place.

"Don't apologize! I *really* need your advice." I ducked my head. "I'm not exactly… used to traveling. In fact, it's kind of a first-time thing for me."

"I've never been south," Isla admitted. Her voice was quiet, but full of curiosity. She rubbed her fingers against the soft lining of a skirt. "All your clothes are so pretty. I've never seen fabrics like this before."

I stared at the clothes and shrugged. "Pretty, but useless."

The only exception was the clothes that had been altered for me that had once been Lucy's, but I didn't see many of those hanging up. Perhaps they were still being transferred here.

Isla frowned with concentration as she scanned through the rack holding my dresses. Eventually she made a noise of victory, pulling out a soft pair of slacks and a sweater from the back.

She handed me the items before stepping back and looking me up and down, assessing.

"Wait here," she said, before turning tail and leaving me holding the garments—and feeling more confused than ever.

I held them up in front of the mirror and smiled. It was hardly my usual style, but maybe I could get used to it. The whole point of the trip was to try new things.

"Winter chic," I whispered to myself. The reflected Cass smiled back at me in the long mirror.

Isla returned with a dust-covered box tucked under one arm.

"I found these tucked away in the old queen's quarters," she said, handing over the box to me.

I took it, puzzled.

"They look about your size... You'll need them if you want to stand a chance on frozen ground."

She stared pointedly at the soft shoes I'd worn yesterday. They hadn't survived the hedge maze; they lay abandoned, still drying out in front of the fireplace. The silk was crumpled, stained with mud.

A flush heated my cheeks.

I brushed away the dust on the box and opened the lid, pulling the soft tissue paper away to reveal a sturdy pair of boots nestled within.

I pulled them out one by one, then plopped down on the armchair and tugged them on over my nightclothes. I felt kind of ridiculous, but wouldn't risk insulting my newfound friend by waiting until later to try them on. Isla had to help with the laces, but pretty soon I had them figured out.

The boots were calf length, soft and supple. They fit me perfectly.

I turned this way and that in front of the mirror, unable to remember the last time I'd worn clothes built for practicality as well as beauty.

It felt surprisingly good.

"They suit you, Your Highness," Isla remarked. "Will you need any help with the rest?"

I shook my head. "I can manage from here, thank you."

As she left the room, I grinned. So far, so good. I dressed and threw my hair back into a simple braid, before hurrying out of the room.

Retracing my steps from the day before turned out to be something of a challenge. After encountering several dead-ends and having an embarrassing run-in with a confused guard, I found myself lingering in the doorway of a huge, darkened chamber.

The dining hall. I peered inside, frowning around at the gloomy space. All the curtains were pulled shut, and the tapestries hanging from the walls were faded and worn.

Guess he doesn't throw many parties in here...

I shut the door softly behind me and crept back along the corridor. Unwilling to ask for help, I ended up following my nose until I came to a standstill outside a room where light spilled out from underneath the closed doors.

Bingo.

I hesitated, and then knocked.

"Come in." Damon's voice traveled through the door. His tone was muffled, but he sounded weary, like he hadn't had much sleep.

Now or never. I turned the handle and slipped over the threshold before I could talk myself out of it.

Damon was sitting behind a huge, old desk. There was only candlelight filling the room with a soft light, and very little else in the room. There was none of the riches I'd come to expect from a kingdom's inner rooms, but this king was like none other.

He looked up at the sound of the door closing behind me. His eyes widened before the blank, stoic mask resettled on his face.

"Cassandra." He stood up, straight-backed and formal.

Okay, so this is how it's gonna go.

"How can I help you?"

"The servants said you don't usually have the chance to stop for breakfast." I bit my lip, noting the way his eyes tracked the motion. "So, I thought I'd come ask if you'd join me?"

He blinked with surprise. There were shadows under his eyes, and thin lines of tension at the corners of his mouth. I ached to know what weighed on him so heavily.

He seemed at a loss for words. "That's very thoughtful of you."

"Thank you." I shot him a smile, edging closer.

I settled for sitting at the edge of his desk, toying at the loose papers strewn over the surface.

"What are you working on?"

"Farming ledgers… it's all boring. Paperwork, mostly," he said, shuffling the papers away out of sight. "I'm heading out to the tenant farms today. I need to see how much grain the kingdom will yield before next winter."

As he spoke, his hands rested on the desk in front of him. They were rough, expressive hands, large and calloused with use. The hands of someone who built things, crafted things. Who worked hard alongside his men. Not a spoilt rich king.

Those same hands that only yesterday had pressed relentlessly into my soft flesh, touched me everywhere, greedy and possessive. I swallowed at the memory, looking away.

"I'd like to come with you, if that's all right?" I said. "I'd like to see more of your kingdom, and meet the people."

Damon ran a hand through his hair, staring at me with a strange look in his eyes. "Are you sure that's what you want?"

I nodded. "Yes, very much so. But with respect, Your Majesty. You need to eat something first."

"Is that so?" he murmured.

The look in his eyes told me he had something else in mind. Another kind of hunger altogether.

Our eyes met. After what felt like an eternity, my cheeks heated, and I ducked my head.

To hide my glowing face, I turned and hurried over to the door, peeking out of it. The footman who waited on the other side looked at me with curiosity.

"His Majesty and I will take breakfast in here this morning," I said, trying to sound confident.

Hell, everyone needs to eat, right? Even the king of the ice dragons!

If the footman was surprised by the request, he didn't show it, merely nodding before turning away. I shut the door and ambled over to a nearby bookshelf.

I felt Damon's eyes burning into my back, tracking my every move.

I didn't turn around, shifting my focus instead to all the unfamiliar titles. I ran my fingers along the decorated spines, my heart pounding in my chest.

Some of the books looked ancient. I burned with curiosity, forgetting myself for a second and sliding free a book with embellished silver wolves on the cover. I leafed through it.

"You like reading?"

The sound of his voice in the hushed room made me jump. Although he hadn't moved from his position at the other side of the desk, the low notes raised goosebumps on the back of my neck, like he was pressed right up against me.

"I do, Your Majesty." I slanted a glance behind me, only to meet his intense gaze.

He looked at me like I was a puzzle he couldn't figure out.

"I didn't have much else to do, growing up."

I said nothing of the loneliness that had carved a deep furrow into my upbringing. My life had been full of music and companionship... but also captivity. Other children were allowed to explore the fields and forests of our kingdom. They roamed free, flying and fighting and playing together from sunrise until sunset.

They weren't afraid of roadside kidnappers. Raiders. Bandits who would gladly hold a young princess for ransom or sell her off to the highest bidder.

Although I didn't say any of this out loud, something in Damon's eyes told me he understood the isolation that came with growing up in a royal house.

I wondered what his own upbringing had been like.

Stavrok told me his father was a tyrant. Is that true?

"Where did you get those?"

I followed the line of his gaze down toward my borrowed boots. "Oh. A maid found them for me. She said I'd need them if I wanted to go out into the fields today."

A shadow crossed over Damon's face. I glanced down at the boots again, feeling awkward. I tilted my head. The look in his eyes had thrown me off.

"I can take them off if you want, Sire?"

"No." He rounded the desk and came to a stop halfway across the room with his arms outstretched.

Before he could reach me, they fell to his sides. I ached for him to come nearer, but he didn't.

"No… I was just…" He frowned. His gaze darted away from mine, settling somewhere on the far wall. "Those boots belonged to my mother."

Oh.

"I'm so sorry," I whispered. "I didn't put it together. I should have asked."

Embarrassment sent me spiraling. What was he going to think of me, rifling through his possessions like that?

He held up a hand. "Please, I won't hear you apologize. You're welcome to them." He paused, staring down at the floor. "It's been a long time since I've seen them, that's all."

His tone was stiff, overly formal, but sincere.

I nodded, still not trusting myself to speak. I wanted to ask him questions—about his mother, his life growing up here—but now wasn't the time. He still looked distracted. He glanced out the window and picked up a handful of papers, shuffling through them, but his eyes were glazed over.

"Cassandra." He was still frowning when he finally addressed me again. "Are you sure you want to go out into the fields today? Wouldn't you rather stay inside the castle, or walk around the rose garden?"

I opened my mouth, but before I could answer him, there was a soft knock at the door. Damon strode over and opened it, and the sweet smell of breakfast drifted in.

I smiled, grateful for the distraction. I slid past him and took the tray from the maid, thanking her, before setting it down on the desk between us.

I picked up a piece of toast and nibbled on it while I considered my answer.

I knew what Damon was trying to do: palm me off on the castle and its grounds, confine me to ladylike pursuits in the hope that I'd be content to wander around exploring every nook and cranny of this place.

Stay inside. Warm and safe.

The thought was tempting, but I knew he had another reason for wanting me out of the way.

He wants to put as much distance between us as possible.

The thought lanced through my heart. I was determined not to give into the pain of it. I wanted Damon to take me seriously. To prove to him that I *could* do this.

Finally, I looked up at him, raising an eyebrow. "When do we leave?"

CHAPTER 8

Cass

The wind howled around us, battering the carriage as it bumped and trundled along over the barren fields. I pressed my face into the collar of my coat, trying not to shiver.

Seemingly unbothered by the cold, Damon rode up ahead on horseback. He made an indistinct, lone figure against the horizon. Only the bare skeletal trees marked the landscape. It was a far cry from the lush orchards and grassy meadows I was used to.

When I confessed that I'd never ridden before, Damon had looked surprised, but he didn't pass comment on it. I guessed it was just another weakness in his eyes, fitting in with his image of the pampered princess flitting around her tower in satin slippers.

I squinted at the farmstead up ahead as we approached. It was a simple building, with cozy-looking gables overhanging the wraparound porch. The farmer and his wife waited for us outside, on the steps. Damon arrived first, and he dismounted, handing off the reins to his footman and striding up to the farmhouse.

I was struck by the way he carried himself. Every line of his body spoke of an easy confidence, commanding, yet open and friendly.

The couple bowed their heads to him, and the farmer struck up a conversation. From their tone of voice, it was clear that Damon knew them well.

All told, it was hard to imagine that this was the same man I'd shared breakfast with. The one who looked at me like a spooked animal and shied away every time I got too close for comfort.

One of Damon's men helped me down from the carriage. I nodded to him, and picked my way over the uneven ground. A deep permafrost made the earth hard and unyielding, and I would have slipped without my borrowed footwear.

The farmer's wife looked at me as I stepped up to join Damon, her eyes widening in astonishment. She sank into a low curtsy, and I smiled at her when she straightened up.

Damon's eyes darted to mine before glancing away again.

"Allow me to present the Princess Cassandra of the Bravdok Clan," he said, as if reading from a script. "She is currently... visiting the castle."

I inclined my head at the couple, silently noting Damon's phrasing. *Visiting.*

Well, if that's how you want to play it...

"It's an honor, Your Highness," the farmer said. Like most of the men in the north, his weather-beaten, heavily lined face spoke of a harsh life. "How long will you be staying with us?"

"As long as I'm welcome here." I smiled back at him. I felt Damon's eyes on me, but didn't look at him. "You see, I've wanted to visit these lands my whole life."

"Well, you're certainly welcome here on our farm." The farmer's wife gave me another warm smile. Her tone was pleasant, but her eyes were burning with curiosity. "And—forgive me for saying so, my king —we're so used to you coming out here alone. It's good to see you with company for a change."

I heard the implication in her words, the way she lingered on *company*, and ducked my head, a blush coming on. I could feel the couple still eyeing me curiously.

Damon cleared his throat. "So. I was glad to receive your letters. I take it you've made progress cultivating the southern fields for livestock?"

"Oh, yes, Sire." The farmer rocked back and forth on his heels before putting out his hand. "Please, follow me…"

As the two men strode off over the field, Damon glanced back at me, just once, like he was checking I was okay. I nodded at him. He turned away, apparently satisfied, resuming his conversation with the farmer.

The farmer's wife was watching me when I turned to look at her. There was a knowing twinkle in her eyes that only grew as her face lifted into a broad smile.

"Would you like some tea, Your Highness?"

I rubbed my hands together, attempting to chase away the chill, and nodded.

She led the way inside, taking me to a comfortable kitchen with a view of the fields out back. It was rustic, simple, not unlike the cabin Stavrok and I had stayed in on our journey here. A fire burned merrily in the grate, and a small copper kettle hung above it.

I relaxed onto a window seat covered with a patchwork quilt. As the woman poured the tea, I traced my finger over the rich patterns, letting myself be comforted by the soft noises of her whistling and the crackle of the fire.

There was so little about this land that I understood. Bravdok seemed like a lifetime away.

I took the teacup from her, before frowning. "I didn't catch your name."

"It's Molly, ma'am." The woman settled in a sturdy armchair and eyed me like she was measuring me up for something. "So. You're to be our new queen?"

I blanched, almost spilling the tea all over myself. I set the cup down on the small table in front of me. "What?"

"Oh, don't worry." Molly gave me a conspiratorial smile. "I saw the way the two of you looked at each other. I know how it goes. When it's meant to be, it's meant to be."

I chewed her words over. She wasn't wrong: my dragon had recognized Damon's immediately. I remembered the way it uncoiled in my chest, reaching out from the moment we laid eyes on each other.

My eyebrows drew together. I looked down into my teacup, like the answers I sought were in there.

"What if it's not that simple?" I whispered.

Maybe it was wrong to spill all my troubles onto the first person to take any interest, but I needed to talk to someone. Hell, I needed *advice.*

Something about this woman told me I could trust her.

"What could be simpler?" Molly cocked her head to the side. Like her husband, she had lines around her eyes, but they were softer, friendlier. *Laugh lines.* "He cares for you. You care for him."

Well. When she put it like that, it *did* sound simple.

"He doesn't even know me," I whispered. Needing something to do with my hands, I picked up the cup, running my fingers along the floral rim.

"But he *will.*"

Molly said it with such certainty, I half-wondered if she, like Marienne, had the gift of sight in her. I sensed it wasn't polite to ask.

I stared blindly out the window. Somewhere out there, Damon was pacing the fields, checking over his ancestral homelands, doing the job he had been born to do.

I pressed a hand to the cup, half-wishing I was out there with him.

I turned back to Molly. "You seem very certain about all this."

"I've lived a long life." She shrugged. "And he is my King."

"Then you must know him," I said, leaning forward again to face her. "Better than me, anyway. Tell me. *Why* is he so..."

Withdrawn? Moody? Unreasonable? Infuriating?

Her mouth quirked with amusement. I flushed, feeling that uncomfortable sensation again.

She can read me like a book.

"His Majesty had... a difficult upbringing," she said carefully.

"In what way?"

"You know of his father, of course."

I nodded. Stavrok had told me about the old king. How he'd

drained his people of money and driven his kingdom into debt. Stavrok and Rage had joined forces with Damon to put an end to the scavengers and raiders who wanted to pillage the north and settle old scores. They hadn't cared how many lives were lost, as long as the debt was paid in blood.

The sins of Damon's father were legendary all over the realm.

"His mother died shortly after his sister was born." Molly frowned into the distance, lost in memories. "It drove the old king mad with grief. They say he was never the same afterwards."

I thought of the look on Damon's face that morning when he'd spoken of his mother.

"Damon's father took his pain out on the whole kingdom." Molly's face darkened. "Crops failed; cattle starved. All the while, he stood by and did nothing. Locked himself away in his castle, growing more paranoid by the day… and the young prince, too."

"Damon?"

"Aye. People barely saw him until his father died, and he became king. By then, the castle was a wreck. There's so much darkness in that place." The woman clicked her tongue. "Bad, bad memories. It's a wonder that he's managed at all."

I stared into space, processing everything she'd said. I tried not to let the shock I felt show on my face.

Despite my overprotective upbringing, I couldn't deny that my life had been full of love. Music and laughter filled my memories when I thought of my childhood. I had a cousin who loved me, and a kingdom that welcomed me with open arms.

It sounded like Damon hadn't been so lucky.

"More tea?" she asked, holding the pot in her hand.

"No, thank you."

Molly smiled at me kindly. "Try not to worry so much, my dear. You'll clear out the cobwebs of that old place, I just know it."

By the time Damon and the farmer arrived at the door, stamping the snow off their boots, I was warmed through. I wandered over to the door to stand by the king. As we turned to leave, Molly dropped into a low curtsy, her eyes twinkling with pleasure.

"You're welcome to drop by whenever you want to, Your Highness," she said, looking directly at me.

I was hyperaware of Damon's presence at my side. His body had brought the cold in with it. He smelled of fresh air and snow. Snowflakes littered his hair and the collar of his dark coat. I jumped at the shock of coldness as his fingers brushed against mine.

Molly's smile grew.

"Thank you," I told her. "For everything."

I FELT DAMON'S EYES ON ME AS WE WALKED BACK TO THE HORSES.

"What?" I quirked an eyebrow in his direction.

"Nothing," he replied, a little too hastily.

I raised both eyebrows, a smile playing at the corners of my mouth.

"You're good at that," he said quietly. He opened his mouth, like he wanted to say more, then closed it again.

Good at what?

I wanted to challenge him, ask him why he was so surprised I could hold a conversation with a farming woman. What kind of girl did he take me for?

But I didn't push him for anything more. I accepted the compliment for what it was.

We came to a standstill by the side of the men, who were holding the carriage horses by the bridles, waiting for me to climb inside. Both of us were lingering, not wanting to be separated just yet. At least, that how I felt. I can only assume he felt the same way.

"Come on." Damon closed his hand around the reins of his horse. He offered his other hand to me, and I took it, though I was confused. He tugged me closer, his large hand gentle around my own. "You ride with me."

Before I could say anything in reply, his hands wrapped around my waist. I gasped at their firmness, and the warmth I could feel even through the layers of outerwear. He boosted me into the air, and I swung my leg over the horse, clutching the mane and panting with shock.

"Oh, my—"

His hand clenched around the horse's bridle, and the animal trembled, huffing a little as Damon climbed up behind me.

Damon exhaled, the motion pressing his chest against my back. He leaned forward, and his breath tickled the side of my neck. I shivered and closed my eyes, knowing he couldn't see how I trembled with desire for him. But I knew.

He clutched the reins, an arm on either side of my waist. Then he spoke into my ear, his voice rumbling straight through me. "Comfortable?"

That's not exactly the word I would use.

I nodded to his question. I didn't trust myself to turn around and give him a response with words. That would bring our faces dangerously close to one another.

He shouted something to his men and clicked the reins together.

And then we were off.

I swallowed the scream that rose as I clung to the saddle in front of me, the huge arms of Damon surrounding me on each side and his body behind.

We thundered over the countryside like the hounds of hell were on our tail. Initially, there was only terror in my heart, but as I relaxed, I began to enjoy the exhilaration of the cold against my face, and the horse beneath me. The blood sang through my veins. Riding with Damon was almost like flying, that same exhilaration, except this time, I wasn't in control. *He* was.

His body crowded close to me. It was impossible to ignore every flex of his thighs behind my ass. Every brush of his arms against my chest as he adjusted our course.

I could barely pay attention to the world around me, or what was going on outside of the feelings inside me. That need was building up again: the need to claim what was mine.

But I knew that wasn't what he wanted.

My mind and body screamed at each other, tortured by the mixed signals. I was powerless to do anything in my current position. I could only let Damon ride us to our destination.

He grunted behind me, and his hand pressed against my belly, pulling me more firmly against his chest. I wanted to arch back into him until I realized that he was merely adjusting my position, making sure I didn't fall.

By the time Damon slowed the horse to a trot, we were coming up to a shallow slope that led down onto a rocky scree. Several wagons had pulled up at the side of the road around us, and there were people everywhere, hard at work digging and toiling in the earth.

"When the raiders came, they burned many homes to the ground," Damon said, speaking for the first time since we started this journey. "My people needed raw materials to rebuild. Stone, mostly."

A team of people manoeuvred a huge machine to the base of the slope. Damon slowed the horse to a standstill. He jumped off with ease and held out a hand for me.

I climbed down more gingerly, running a shaky hand over the horse's mane.

"Thank you," I whispered to the horse. "Sorry for being nervous of you before."

Just before he turned away, I saw the edge of a smile on Damon's face and my heart lifted at the hope that twisted within my chest.

CHAPTER 9

amon

My heart was still pounding heavily beneath my shirt as I approached my men.

I'd regretted my foolish impulse to ride with Cass as soon as I felt her small frame in my arms. She'd been so distracting I'd struggled with the simple task of leading the horse in the right direction. The scent of her hair, the softness of her thighs pressed up against mine… It was all far too tantalizing.

Pull yourself together.

The voice inside my head, cold and stoic, sounded remarkably like my father.

He was probably right. I couldn't afford distractions, not today. *Not any day.*

I let out a deep sigh and walked on.

Cass trotted up alongside me as we drew closer to the stone quarry. "Can I walk down there and get a closer look?"

I shook my head, frowning at the very idea that she'd wander off exploring. "You need to keep close to me."

Several of the men put down their tools as we approached, giving her a furtive once-over glance as they did so. My hackles rose as my possessive instinct pulsed through me. I clenched my jaw and forced myself to keep walking.

I ached to take her far away from them. I wanted to shift and fly us both back to the castle, just to get her out of their sight. There, I would claim her all over again, leaving her gasping my name until she could barely remember her own.

I am their king. Nobody will hurt her. Nobody will touch her. She is safe.

The mantra did little to calm me down. My dragon was inflamed and the men seemed to notice, because they dropped their gazes, mumbling amongst themselves.

I drew level with them. "Is it ready?"

"Yes, Sire." Jace, my well-built foreman, spoke up. "We're waiting for your go-ahead."

I nodded. "Very well, then. Fire away."

Cass looked up at me curiously as we strode toward the edge of the rocky slope. I bent closer, letting my mouth almost brush against her ear.

The quarry is so noisy; she won't be able to hear me otherwise.

It was a flimsy excuse at best. Luckily, if she noticed the way I wasn't breathing normally, she didn't say anything.

"We drilled down into the side of the rock yesterday. Now we're packing it with explosives," I said. "It's the best way to break up the stone."

As I drew away, a shiver ran through her slender frame. It was no wonder. A chill wind was buffeting us, and the sky once again threatened snow.

"Are you cold?" I asked. Worry sharpened my tone so when I spoke again, I made sure it was softer. "Because I'll take you back to the castle, if you want. You only have to say the word."

Her eyes flashed up to mine. "No! I…"

Before she could continue, a loud whistle broke through the air.

I grabbed her by the arm and pulled her into my body for protection. "Cover your ears. Quickly."

She did so, just as a loud *boom* shook the ground beneath us. Rubble rained down. The men cheered, and I smiled proudly.

Where there had been a huge shelf of rock, there was now a slope, leading to a stone-filled crevice. My men descended into the new quarry, carrying their tools with them and setting to work.

"What now?" she asked, lowering her hands from where they'd been pressed against her ears.

I scrambled down the slope after them. She followed me, surprisingly nimble, ignoring the hand that I held out for her. My mouth quirked at her stubbornness.

"Now, we break up the larger pieces of rock for transport back to the town."

"We?" Cass tilted her head. She watched as I shrugged off my coat and rolled up my shirtsleeves.

"Of course." I smiled. "What kind of king doesn't get into the trenches and dig alongside his men? I'm their leader. I'm hardly going to stand on the sidelines while they do all the work."

I watched her absorb my words.

"In that case," she said, jutting out her chin, "neither am I."

I could already see that there would be no arguing with her, and since I'd all but given her the lines to use against me, why would I bother fighting her? She at least wore pants, and my mother's boots provided protection for her feet.

"Very well, then. Let's get to work."

For the next few hours, we worked in the quarry, picking away at the fragments of rock that lay around us. I showed Cass how to look for the highest quality stone, and she soon began working alongside the men in the processing section, talking with them as if she'd been doing this for years.

The now-familiar bond between us *insisted* I keep a close eye on things. I didn't want her to think I was hovering, but I hated to leave her alone amongst all those men. In fact, I *couldn't* leave her alone, no matter how many times I tried to walk away. It didn't matter that I knew rationally she wasn't in danger.

My dragon didn't give a damn.

I mostly hung around in the background, trying and mostly failing to concentrate on the task at hand.

Jace sidled up to me. The two of us worked well together, and I trusted him implicitly.

He nodded toward the group. "She's in her element out there."

I couldn't help but agree. Watching Cass working with my people stoked a fire inside my chest. It was impossible to keep on task. I could have watched her all day, a small, bright butterfly flitting around all those hardened men like she was born to it.

"If you don't mind me saying so, Sire…" Jace paused for a long time. He was usually a man of few words. I tilted my head, curious. "It's good to see a smile on your face."

I wasn't even aware I *was* smiling.

"Oh. Thank you Jace," I managed to say, then turned back to look at the little princess I'd been worried would never fit in here.

But watching her out here, it began to dawn on me that I may have misjudged her. She wasn't afraid to get her hands dirty… literally. I'd given her the option of staying at the castle, cozy and warm by the fireside, and instead she was out here working on the frozen tundra with me.

She turned her head, and my breath caught at the sight she made. A curly strand of hair pulled loose from her braid, floated in the wind and brushed along her cheek, unnoticed. She had a smudge of dirt on the tip of her nose.

When she caught my eye, I realized I was staring, but she didn't seem to mind. She gave me a small smile and I couldn't help but smile back. I inclined my head, giving her a stiff nod, and got back to work.

At midday, when a weak sun shone above us in the pale gray sky, I called a halt to the work. Cass and I sat on a rocky outcrop, a little apart from the others, and passed pieces of a sourdough loaf between us in comfortable silence.

"I'm sure you're used to fancier fare," I mumbled, fingering a scrap of the coarse bread.

I was used to this, but Cass had grown up surrounded by beauty and luxury. Through her eyes, I saw the northern way of life in a new light.

We must look like barbarians to her…

To my surprise, she only shrugged. "I've always preferred bread and cheese to huge elaborate dinners." A dreamy expression crossed her face. "Although, I do miss strawberries."

I laughed. "Good luck finding those up here." I put out my hand, catching a few drifting snowflakes in the palm of my hand. It was snowing lightly again. "I can't recall the last time I ate one."

Her answering laughter was a soothing melody to my ears. I couldn't help but turn to her. My hand came out, unbidden, and I brushed off the snow that had settled on her shoulder.

She leaned into my touch, seemingly unconscious of the gesture.

"Come on," I found myself saying. "I have to show you something

ass

This time, I was expecting the horse ride, which made it a little bit easier to handle.

But only a little.

My legs were still trembling by the time Damon dismounted. He didn't offer me a hand. Instead, he simply caught me around the waist and lifted me down. I swayed into him when he set me on the ground and for a moment I forgot where we were.

He felt so good against me. Solid and warm. I wanted to lean into his strength, and stay there forever.

He seemed to need a moment to gather himself too, because he didn't move away very quickly.

"So," I began, and as I spoke, I was surprised to hear the husky undertones in my voice. "What did you want to show me?"

Instead of answering, he merely took my hand. There was a tantalizing mystery in his eyes, and I couldn't help but be drawn toward it. We weren't on the open plains anymore. High rocks loomed above us, and a pale, watery sun shone in the sky above.

"Come with me." He winked at me, apparently determined to be mysterious.

I rolled my eyes but let him lead me down the narrow mountain track we were on. The air felt warmer here, probably sheltered from the harsh elements by the hills around us.

Odd patches of greenery grew in amongst the rocky terrain. It was the first true sign of nature I'd seen since arriving in the north. The sight warmed my heart.

"Damon." I squeezed his hand, drawing his attention. "Where *are* we?"

"You'll have to wait and see."

I trotted along beside him, trying to match his long strides. Curiosity burned within me, mingling with the ache that had taken up residence in the pit of my stomach.

I need him. So much. How does he not feel the same way?

I was almost frightened at the strength of my feelings, despite knowing that they were due to the mating bond. I wondered if I'd always feel this burning pull, this *desire* that colored every interaction with this man and made it impossible to stay away.

It was my dragon who felt it most. But that desire, that need, had grown bigger now. It was more than just pure, naked *want*.

I'd never felt this way before. When his eyes met mine, my stomach swooped like I'd missed a step on a staircase.

Maybe I should've asked Stavrok more questions...

I dismissed the thought. There was no way I was talking to Stavrok about any of this! He'd already seen more than enough as it was.

Damon stopped in the middle of the path. He bent his head, and I shivered as his mouth brushed the edge of my ear. Did he know the effect he had on me?

"Do you trust me?" he whispered.

The words took me back to our encounter in the maze. The first words we'd properly spoken to each other. A spark of heat had passed between us then, just as it did now.

"Yes," I breathed.

Sheer instinct spoke for me, but as soon as I said it, I realized it was true.

He'll protect me. He won't let any harm come to me.

They were exhilarating thoughts.

He stepped behind me, and his palms came up to cover my eyes. I could barely breathe as he guided me forward.

I felt like I was on the edge of a precipice, about to fall.

It was the best goddamn feeling in the world.

Soon enough, we came to a standstill. His hands fell away, and I opened my eyes.

I gasped.

We stood in the middle of a lush, green valley. The rocks underfoot were carpeted in moss, and the hillside around us was scattered with flowers. There was running water nearby and I soon spotted a mountain spring trickling down from the rockface.

In the middle of such a barren, frozen land, it was like I'd fallen into a dream.

I turned to Damon. The astonishment must have shown on my face because he huffed out a pleased laugh.

The stiffness in his shoulders was gone, and the color had returned to his face.

"What is this place?" I whispered.

"A secret hideaway." His mouth flickered with amusement, but his eyes were soft. He put his hands in his pockets, surveying our surroundings. "I come here sometimes, to get away from..."

He trailed off, but I caught his drift. To get away from the palace. From his father. From his responsibilities. His life.

The crown weighed heavily on him. This place was his solace, a temporary respite from the stresses of day-to-day life.

"Who else knows about it?"

"Nobody," Damon murmured. "It's my place. And now yours, Cass."

Oh... my...

The thought that he'd led me here, to his private hideout, overwhelmed me. To cover my rising blush, I turned away from him, drawn in by the sound of the water. I sat down beside the small waterfall, feeling the heat of Damon as he came up behind me. My skin tingled at his proximity, yearning for his touch.

"You can drink from this stream," he said, leaning over me and dipping his fingers into the clear stream. I watched, oddly transfixed by the motion. "The water comes directly from the mountain. It's totally pure."

I scooped a handful of water and held it to my lips. It tasted sweet and fresh, just as he said.

"How does this place..." I cast around, searching for the right words. "How does this exist?"

Damon sat back and ran a hand through his hair. He'd taken off his jacket, and my eyes were drawn to the flex of his forearms as he relaxed back onto his elbows.

"I've thought about it." He frowned. "I think the rockface forms a kind of natural shelter from the ice and snow. It protects these plants and gives them a chance at life. Outside, they would just wither away and die, like everything else that tries to grow here."

As he spoke, he plucked a stray daisy beside him and leaned over, threading it through the ends of my braid.

It was a sad thought. I ran a hand over the daisy, fiddling with it.

"So, it's only here because it's protected?"

"I guess so."

From the weather, and the rest of the world. If everyone knew about this place, it would surely be trashed within a few weeks.

I let my hand dangle in the edge of the stream. I watched the flow of water before something else occurred to me.

"But I've seen fields. People farm here, don't they?"

Damon frowned. "They farm the tough plants. Root vegetables. Things that can survive the frost, not delicate flowers like these. Our crops are hardly beautiful. They're just tough."

"Maybe they're beautiful *because* they're tough."

Damon didn't look convinced. "Maybe."

It seemed like a pointless argument. Anyway, we weren't really talking about the vegetation anymore. I huffed out a sigh.

Flopping onto my back, I tilted my head toward him. "You're quite stubborn, do you know that?"

He snorted. "*I'm* stubborn?"

His playful tone emboldened me.

"Yes." I reached out and wrapped my fingers around his forearm, tugging gently.

I hope I'm playing this right...

He came willingly, crawling up over me until his arms were either side of my head.

"I can't fight this, Cass." His eyes burned into mine. "No matter what I do, I can't."

"Then stop trying," I whispered.

He lowered his head and pressed his lips against mine.

I returned the kiss eagerly, wrapping a hand around the back of his neck to bring him even closer. He inhaled sharply, and I smiled against his mouth.

With a shock, I realized that it was the first time we'd kissed.

In the cave, it had been all fire and lust. We'd been strangers then, drawn together by our bodies' urges. This time it was different. Slower. Softer.

We were taking our time with each other. He trailed his lips beyond my mouth, kissing behind my ear, and I moaned with a sudden, unexpected burst of pleasure.

His hands skimmed over my body and peeled off the winter layers one by one. He moved like he was handling something precious, as if I might break with one wrong move.

Eventually I grew impatient and dragged him back on top of me, digging my heels into the small of his back to get him where I wanted him.

He growled, and the light of his dragon burned in his eyes.

It was tempered this time though—a burning ember rather than a roaring flame.

His fingers curved over my side and brushed against my inner thighs. He ducked his head and pressed a burning kiss into the hollow of my throat, against my collarbone, between my breasts, down onto my stomach.

My face heated once I realized his intention, but I didn't stop him from exploring my body further. I reached out a shaking hand to thread my fingers through his hair, and he looked up.

His eyes met mine, our gazes clashing together with the ring of steel against steel. Against our lush surroundings, Damon's eyes were even paler than normal, like shards of ice.

Whatever he saw on my face, he seemed satisfied, because his head dropped again and I arched up at the sudden hot press of his mouth against my hip.

I bit my lip, but I couldn't stop the moan that escaped me as his mouth skated across my inner thigh.

He hadn't even reached his destination yet, and already my voice was wrecked.

When his tongue found my clit, I groaned. My legs clenched over his shoulders, and I trembled at the roughness of his stubble against the soft skin of my thighs. He circled the sweet spot for several delirious minutes until I was bucking up into him, fingers alternately grasping against the mossy bank and raking through his hair in turn.

I wailed as my orgasm crashed over me. He carried me through it, tasting me greedily, buried between my thighs until the sensation was too much and I was forced to drag him up.

We kissed deeply and my face burned at the thought of where his mouth had just been, but I couldn't dwell on it. I had another goal in mind.

My legs came up again, wrapping themselves around his waist, and I raked my hand up underneath his shirt.

He seemed to get the message. He sat back on his haunches, stripping quickly before settling back down over me. I was still hazy from my climax, and I blinked up at him, taking in the set of his jaw and the clench of his muscled arms on either side of me.

Something hard trailed down against my chest, and I blinked lazily. I caught a flash of metal glinting in the light as he tossed it over his shoulder, out of the way. It was a chain of some sort, with something on the end of it…

I was too distracted to think on it further. His hot weight was finally against me, and his hard length pressed against my inner thigh. I trembled.

"I need you," I murmured, reaching down and taking his cock in my hand.

He sucked in a sharp breath, and his head dropped onto my shoulder. He mumbled something unintelligible before looking up again, his normally icy pale eyes now almost black with arousal.

"The things you do to me, Cass…"

We both groaned as he slid inside me.

The fire, the need I'd felt in the cave was still there; it always would be, I realized, whenever we were joined like this. Our dragons were greedy for each other, and the heat inside my chest only increased when I caught a glimpse of Damon's shifter in the burn of his gaze.

"So beautiful…" Damon stroked the hair back from my face. His blunt, broad fingers traced over my cheek, the bud of my lips.

He looked at me like I was a priceless jewel. Like he couldn't believe what he was doing.

I surged up and caught his mouth in a kiss. Our tongues brushed against each other as he rode into me, and before long I felt a second orgasm building. With every thrust of his hips he pushed me closer to the edge.

This time though, he was right there with me. As I dug my fingernails into his arms, crying out as my orgasm pulsed through me, he growled, chasing my climax, thrusting into me faster, deeper, before spilling hotly inside of me.

He brushed the tangled hair from my forehead, and pressed a final kiss onto my damp, heated skin.

Sweet oblivion.

For the first time in a long time, I felt truly at peace. The mossy bank under me was pillow-soft, and the gentle flow of water lulled my senses.

Damon settled down beside me. He folded an arm over my chest, and his breathing slowed. He felt so safe.

I reached out blindly, pressing my hand to his chest to feel the comforting *thud* of his heartbeat.

My eyes fluttered closed, and I drifted off to sleep.

Damon

"Cass," I whispered. "Cass, it's time to go."

She curled closer into me, mumbling something in her sleep I didn't catch. I smiled and kissed the top of her head, turning my face upwards to the rocky sky.

It was late afternoon now. The days were long here, but the nights were even longer: soon it would be dark, and we needed to find the workers and return to the castle before it became impossible to navigate.

"Cass," I said again, more firmly this time.

Finally, her eyelashes fluttered, and her eyes fixed hazily on mine.

"Come on, sleepyhead."

We found our clothes, pulling them on. The temperature had dropped considerably since we'd arrived in the clearing, and I moved closer to her, turning up the collar of her coat to keep the chill away.

Her fingers paused on the buttons of her coat. She reached out, one finger running down the chain that lay partly exposed under the neck of my shirt.

"What's this?"

I glanced down at her wandering fingers, enjoying the sensation on my skin, before stepping away. I tucked the chain away and buttoned up my coat properly. The metal seemed to burn my skin through the fabric, like a beacon.

"Nothing important," I murmured. "Just a family heirloom."

She seemed to accept this, although the tilt of her eyebrow told me she'd get the truth out of me sooner or later. Her expression was still questioning.

"What changed your mind?"

I was caught off-guard by the sudden topic change. "About what?"

She lifted her chin, putting her hands on her hips. "About me."

I just stood there, wracking my brain over what to say. She didn't seem bothered by my pause. She waited, both eyebrows raised.

I'd been in a tailspin all day, determined to keep my distance yet unable to resist her sweet allure. But it was more than that.

She doesn't miss a trick, this one. That's for sure.

"You did well today," I said eventually. "My people don't take kindly to outsiders. Today, at the farmhouse, and at the quarry, you won them over. You're... not what I expected."

Cass shook her head, like I'd amused her in some way. "I'm used to talking to people who find my status intimidating. The guardsmen back home. The servants. I grew up in the palace so I know they find me hard to relate to. But I try my best to make them see me as a person, and if not, a distraction, right?" She shrugged. "Something to lighten the mood."

I frowned. That wasn't the case at all.

"That's not true." I came over to stand in front of her. I reached out and took her hands in mine, forcing her to meet my eye. "You want to know what I think? I think they saw a queen."

Cass looked up at me. Her eyes were shining, but her face was smooth and calm.

I drew up her hand and kissed it.

The gesture was overly formal, considering what we'd just done, but it felt right. I was giving her the respect that should have been afforded to her the first time we met. A princess's welcome.

Before our shifters got in the way.

They were gone, for now, sated by the pleasure we'd just drowned ourselves in. My dragon slept lazily inside my chest, content to have his mate close by.

We stood there in the twilight. I leaned down to brush a loose strand of hair off her face. When I straightened up, she was still regarding me. Chin up, shoulders back.

Anyone in the realm, down to the lowliest kitchen boy, could have seen the royal blood flowing through her in that moment.

A sharp whistle from somewhere beyond the rocks caught my attention.

We had been gone too long. My men had sent out a search party to look for us.

"Come on," I said.

She tucked herself into my side easily, and together we picked our way through the valley, emerging on the other side of the rocks.

I strode over to untie my horse, but we didn't have time to get into the saddle. Lanterns bobbed through the dusk, casting long shadows over the rockface around them.

"Over here!" I waved, and the lanterns drew closer.

"Sire." Jace, who was leading the men, hurried forward, his relief plain across his face. "We thought the raiders had come."

A flicker of regret passed through me as I caught a couple of worried looks from others in the group.

My people were fearful for good reason. The mountain-dwellers that had ransacked our kingdom two years earlier were still out there somewhere. We had thinned their ranks, but that didn't mean they were gone for good.

They were biding their time, hungry for revenge.

"No, nothing like that," I said. "Cass and I just wanted to... explore."

Judging by the expression on Jace's face, I could tell that he knew exactly the kind of *exploring* I meant, but thankfully he didn't remark on it.

He took my horse's bridle and led it toward the search party. They were all waiting in a huddle, their bulky shadows looming over the gravel terrain.

After spending all afternoon with Cass, the contrast between her and my kinsmen was even more pronounced. She stood at least half a foot below the shortest of them, but she greeted them like old friends, dragging me along with her. They were careful not to get too close to her, obviously fearing my dragon.

We set off. The terrain was too unstable to go on horseback, so we had to travel on foot. We climbed down the rocky slope in tandem. I barely thought about where I was putting my feet. I'd spent years walking over these rocks.

Cass picked her way over the ground carefully. I pointed out the sturdiest stones for her and guided her around the deadly black ice that lay in wait of unsuspecting travelers.

Then Cass spotted Rob, the kind, elderly man she had been working with earlier that day, and she was off like a rocket.

Before I could stop her, she'd slithered halfway down the slope in front of us in order to catch up with him. I'd only taken my eyes off her for one second, just enough time for her to dart ahead of me, out of reach.

A sharp cry echoed through the valley.

Cass. My stomach plummeted sickeningly.

I broke into a run and shouldered aside a couple of concerned bystanders before dropping onto my knees beside Cass. She was curled up against a rock, cradling her ankle in her hands.

Gently, I pried off her fingers and ran my hands over the skin, pulling away when she grimaced with pain.

"It's just a sprain." She looked up at me. "Damon. Come on. I'll be *fine.*"

Her words were soothing, but I could tell she was in pain. For some reason, she seemed more concerned with *me* than the injury.

I turned her foot slightly to look at the side of her leg and she winced. There was a rip in her pants, and blood stained the thick material.

"Is that…" I reached out and touched the wet patch, and stared down at my hands.

Cass's bright red blood coated my fingers. I swallowed hard, my dragon roaring inside my head.

"One of the rocks just cut me a bit," she said. "I'm a shifter. I'll be fine. You know that."

I couldn't concentrate on any of her words, or the calm energy she was trying to push toward me. All around me, the noise of the men murmuring amongst themselves buzzed through my head, growing louder and louder. Nobody got too close, but they set my teeth on edge, nonetheless.

"Leave us!" I barked.

I had never spoken in anger like that before. I startled them, but I didn't care.

My men obeyed, and we were alone. Only the wind whistling against the rocks around us broke the silence.

I stroked my hands over Cass's hair until we were both calmer. Eventually, Cass looked up at me.

"You shouldn't have done that." Her mouth turned down at the edges. "I'm okay, really."

"You're *not* okay. You're hurt."

A voice in the back of my mind pulsed like a drumbeat.

This is all my fault. I brought her out here, into danger… and now look what's come of it.

My rational side insisted I was taking it too far. The injury wasn't bad—she just wasn't used to the terrain—but I didn't listen to it.

In that moment, I wasn't King Damon.

There was only the dragon inside me, snarling and helpless, confronted with its injured mate—and ready to lash out at any threat, real or imagined, that got too close.

I helped her to sit up, but when I put my arms under her to carry her the rest of the way her body stiffened against mine.

"I can walk just fine on my own." She glared up at me. "You don't need to act like I'm going to break."

I sat back on my heels, stung by the force of her words. "Cass, you're being unreasonable."

"No." Her eyes flashed with anger. "I'm not. You think I haven't noticed how you treat me?"

I ducked my head, but I wasn't about to back down now.

"You can't walk on that ankle," I said, reasonably enough. "You'll only injure it further."

I gazed down at her slender legs, sprawled out against the rocks. She was so beautiful, so perfect.

So soft.

She couldn't survive in this place.

In that moment, my mind was made up. I would rather spend the rest of my life knowing that she was safe before I let anything happen to her…even if that meant I could never see her again.

Ignoring my warnings, Cass struggled to her feet. She leaned on her side, obviously favoring her uninjured ankle, but I didn't dare touch her.

She put her hands on her hips. "Why can't you accept that I *want* to be here, Damon? That I want to stay?"

I threw out my hands. "Why would you *want* to spend the rest of your life somewhere like this?"

"Because *you're* here!" Petite as she was, Cass had a way of making her presence felt, like no other woman I'd ever known.

I took a step back, struck by the force of her words.

"I know how I feel, Damon. And I know how *you* feel. The bond between us—"

"I don't care about the bond! All I care about is keeping you safe." I ran a hand over my face, suddenly exhausted. "And I can't do that by letting you shackle yourself to me."

"What are you trying to say?" Cass's face was inches from mine. Her eyes were full of tears.

"That you should never have come here!" My voice echoed over the empty landscape, reverberating off the barren gray rocks. "This place will destroy you. Just as it did my mother."

As soon as I said it, I wanted to take it back.

"You're a coward," she whispered. Her eyes were still glassy, but hard. "You're ready to give up. On me. Even after what we've shared. I thought you were better than that."

I felt the blood drain from my face.

It's not like that, I wanted to say.

I didn't know how to make her understand. I wasn't rejecting her.

"Cass, I—"

I reached out to her. She ducked out of reach, turning her back on me, and limped away.

My dragon grumbled inside my chest, but I ignored it.

This is all your fault, Damon.

The air shimmered around Cass's form, and my heart almost stopped.

"Cass! No!"

It was too late. Cass shifted in front of me, and I saw her dragon for the first time.

She was slender, and smaller than shifters tended to be this far north. As her wings extended, they shimmered pale violet. She turned to look at me one last time, and with a flash of her jewel-like eyes, she launched herself into the sky.

I could only look on in shock as she flew off into the distance. Each beat of her wings broke something inside my chest. She was flying away from me. Leaving me. Going home to where she'd be safe.

Despair filled me as she climbed higher and higher, edging further toward the forest in the foothills of the mountains.

Then, out of nowhere, two dragons swooped out from the thick bank of cloud that wreathed the mountaintop.

"No!"

I didn't recognize those dragons. They weren't my people.

They divebombed Cass on either side, releasing twin jets of ice on her as she twisted and thrashed her wings to get away from them.

My dragon lifted up inside me and I began to shift, keeping my eyes on the sky above me.

Hang on Cass. Hang on. I'm coming.

It was no use. The ambush was short, and swift. I could only watch as Cass's wings folded around her, and she dropped out of the sky like a stone.

CHAPTER 12

Cass

I hit the earth with a thud that would have broken every bone in my body if I hadn't been in my dragon form.

Staring helplessly up at the thick canopy of leaves above me, I could only lie there as I felt my shifter curl up inside my chest. Damn it. I couldn't sustain it.

Soon enough I was human again, naked and shivering in the freezing cold of the north. I curled onto my side and crossed my arms over my chest, closing my eyes.

If I fall asleep, maybe I'll wake up and this will all have been a dream...

With a groan, I opened my eyes again.

I couldn't fall asleep, not now.

But moving *hurt*.

My attackers had damaged my wings, and the pain stung through my body, especially my arms and each side of my ribs. They ached like I'd been punched repeatedly.

Before I could consider my next move, the undergrowth rustled, and sharp voices pierced through.

"— saw her fall down here somewhere. We can't return without the girl."

My heartbeat picked up as I realized they were talking about me.

I squealed as something hot and wet dragged along the side of my face. Terror filled me as I rolled over, only to come face to face with the jaws of a huge wolf.

"Here! She's over here!" a man called out.

Footsteps trampled over the ground toward me, and I was surrounded. Hands reached out for my naked body. I tried to bat them away, but they easily caught hold of my wrists. I was totally outnumbered. On all sides of me, tall men with long, shaggy furs loomed over me, holding leashes on the creatures that had haunted my nightmares since I was a little girl: giant wolves.

I began to shake and tremble. Blessedly, a fur was thrown over my shoulders, partially covering me from the cold and the gazes of the men.

I pulled the fur around me and my lip wobbled. What were they going to do to me?

"Scream all you want," the leader of the men told me with a broad grin. "Nobody will hear you out here."

That didn't stop me.

I screamed all the way through the forest and beyond.

DAMON

One moment I was staring up at the sky, feet planted firmly on the ground, and the next I was soaring high over the clouds. I let out an earth-shattering roar of rage as I climbed higher and higher, beating my wings against the howling wind.

Cass! I could feel my mate slipping away from me, somewhere far below, in the forest at the edge of the horizon.

In the distance, a pale shape rose above the trees. My heart skipped, and for a brief second, I thought she'd managed to fight off the attackers and was free.

When a second dragon flew up to join the first, my hope vanished. It was them. The monsters who had taken her. *Hurt* her.

She was gone.

Muscles straining, I pounded my wings through the air. The wind had turned. While Cass had sped through the air, I was forced to fight through a gathering storm.

My rage urged me onwards, the anger that pumped through my body so strong I could have broken any barrier. The gates of hell could have opened beneath me, and I wouldn't have batted an eye.

Beneath the sheer fury of the dragon, my mind whirled with panic.

What if Cass is dead?

It was my fault, all my fault. I'd put her in harm's way. If she was dead… I couldn't live with myself. I couldn't live. Period.

The ground passing beneath me flooded with greenery, and I wheeled in mid-air, realizing I'd reached the edge of the forest.

I reared up, beating my wings against the sky and letting out a roar. An icy jet of blue fire shot out from my throat.

Come and get me, you bastards.

I caught a flicker of movement in the forest canopy, the edge of a wing sticking out of the trees below.

I dove through the branches, like a hawk spotting a mouse. I caught the dragon in my talons and we tumbled down to the earth together, crashing through branches and bushes.

The forest was cool and dark. The density of the trees dimmed the light, and I staggered backwards, struggling to get my bearings. I was still in dragon form, and wouldn't shift back. Not until my mate was by my side once again.

My anger and panic turned me clumsy and my claws raked the ground, trying to get a foot hold. I blinked in the unfamiliar, greenish light, panting hard. This wasn't my terrain. I was used to open tundra, frozen and unforgiving though it was. The trees above pressed down, trapping me in a cage.

A sharp pain lanced over my back as the enemy shifter dropped down on me from above.

I roared in fury and lashed out, blasting a patch of foliage nearby and reducing it to ice. My blast managed to catch the edge of the shifter's wing, stunning him long enough for me to roll over, shake him off, and send him flying.

The sharp talons at the edges of my wings gave me an advantage, as did my size. Whoever this shifter was, I stood at least two feet taller. Not to mention my wingspan, which dwarfed his own.

His scales, however, were a pale icy color. Just like mine. *Were we kin?*

I couldn't think about that. Not now. Cass was in danger; nothing mattered beyond that.

The fight was vicious and short. The red haze that swirled through my veins turned me merciless; cold blooded. I lashed out, sharp talons tearing through scales, and before long, my opponent lay dead at my feet.

I stood over him, panting.

The bushes trembled. A low, deadly growl sounded. I froze.

Another dragon. This one was bigger and, when he emerged, the undergrowth rustled on either side of him. Yellow eyes came forward, followed by huge paws, soundless and graceful over the forest floor.

Beside the dragon, stood a wolf. Huge and powerful, its hackles were up, lips pulled back to expose its long white teeth. His unblinking gaze fixed on me, waiting for me to make my move.

Another wolf appeared, then another. Before I knew it, the clearing was full of them.

And I was in the center.

This was an ambush.

The shifter's gaze flicked to the dead dragon at my feet. I lowered my head, muscles coiled with tension.

Logically, I knew there were too many of them to fight. My dragon didn't care. Inside, I was roaring, screaming for my mate. And if it couldn't get to her, well, then I'd get to those who stood in my way.

I lunged at the shifter, knocking him to the ground. We tousled, each fighting for our lives. There were sharp jabs against my hide as dozens of wolves piled on us. The air was thick with fur, and blood, and hide, and teeth. We twisted over each other and I snapped at every creature that came at me.

The shifter took advantage of my distraction, snapping at my tail, raking sharp talons over my wings until I scorched the ground in fury.

But any shifter, no matter how powerful, was no match for me.

I was a Dragon King.

And I had a mission.

I drew in a deep breath and *roared.*

The air filled with white ice flames. The blast knocked back the beasts that climbed my flanks, carving a deep crevice in the earth.

By the time I was done obliterating the area, the dragon shifter was dead.

Yet still more wolves were coming. There was a long, low whistle through the trees. I staggered to my feet, bleeding, injured, and exhausted.

If I stayed, I would die.

More shifters would come. This wasn't a battle I could win. Not today. And not on my own. I needed my people. I needed my army.

Frustration clawed its way up my throat, and I considered throwing caution to the wind and pushing through my fear, slaughtering everyone in my path until I found Cass.

But a small voice, a mere echo in the back of my mind—the part that was still human—said, *Damon, no. You're smarter than that. We need reinforcements.*

I hated that voice, but I couldn't argue with it.

If I wanted Cass back safe, I had to be smart.

Cursing the name of every god I could think of, I launched myself back into the sky.

Cass

I sat on the ground in some godforsaken corner of a cell-type prison room, curled up beneath the furs they'd thrown into the room with me. At least I wasn't going to freeze to death.

I stifled a sob against the crook of my arm.

I was scared out of my mind. At least none of them had tried to hurt me. Not yet, anyway.

I wish I'd never come here.

I wish I was home. Somewhere warm, where everyone knows me and no-one would ever try to hurt me like this...

I clenched my jaw, willing the faint spark inside me, the shifter that was currently nothing but a shadow, to warm my chest.

Pull yourself together. You are Cassandra of Clan Bravdok, and you are better than this. You wanted adventure, didn't you? Well, you've got it now.

In all those books you read about the north... what did those explorers do, when they were in a life-or-death situation?

"Found their resources," I muttered to myself.

It wasn't much, but it was a direction at least, a momentary chance to make myself feel a little less powerless.

I managed to lift my head and take stock of my surroundings.

I couldn't see much now. There wasn't any light inside my prison cell, but through the gaps in the walls, the flickering torchlight gave me enough sight to make out the dim interior of a hut.

The walls were made of rough-hewn wood, and the floor was one step above dirt. Whoever my captors were, they weren't advanced.

Or maybe they just don't plan on keeping me here for long.

I pushed away the unhelpful thought and uncurled my legs, stretching out. They hadn't bothered to tie me up, which I took as another clue that they didn't expect me to be able to run away.

I could try to shift, attack them, or fight my way out of here. But these men were ice dragons and had taken me out of the sky once already today. I didn't want to die, and since they didn't seem to want to kill me, I would bide my time and save my strength in case I needed to fight my way out in the end.

The door swung open and a shaft of orange light filtered through, startling me. I ducked as something was thrown at me, but when it landed on the floor with a soft *thud* I realized what it was.

"Get dressed," someone said, just out of view behind me. Then the person slammed the door and I was alone again.

I crawled toward the dark pile, fingers closing around the cloth. It was soft to the touch, but spun out of simple fibers.

I didn't care. I would've worn a freshly stripped wolf pelt in that moment. My hands were stiff as I slipped on the tunic and pulled up the supple leggings.

My final garment, a loosely knitted shrug, was wholly unfamiliar to me, but I slipped it on. Mercifully, the shivering began to ease as I warmed up, and in turn my mind grew clearer.

I shuffled around the small cell, the blood pumping through my veins and reaching my arms and legs. Everything hurt from the cold, but thanks to my shifter blood, I was healthy and well. The small injury I'd sustained before I left Damon and the few scrapes from my fall had healed.

They haven't tied me up, and they've given me clothes... What kind of raiders are these?

A dark thought occurred to me. If I was being held for ransom, I'd be no use to them dead.

I paced faster around the edge of my small enclosure, checking for weak spots on every inch of the walls. My cage was well-built, and from the sounds by the door, I had guards.

I found a gap in the wood big enough to peer through. I caught glimpses of a few people sitting around the fireside, talking amongst themselves.

My heart clenched as three women carried their children across to sit beside the flames. They looked sleepy, but relaxed and content.

It was hardly the stuff of nightmares.

My spying was rudely interrupted by the sound of the deadbolt sliding back from the door, and light spilling through the gap.

I whirled, my fists clenched. I'd never physically fought anyone in my life before, but I wasn't going to cower in the corner like they wanted me to.

"What's going on?" I hissed. "Where the hell am I?"

The man merely looked at me, blank-faced.

"Your Highness," he said. "Come with me."

CHAPTER 13

*D*amon

By the time I found my way back to the castle, the sky had faded into a purplish hue, and a canopy of stars glittered overhead. I had no time to stop and appreciate their beauty. The flight had calmed my mind and body, and as I landed, my mind was clear. My rescue plan had formed. All that remained was to set it into motion.

I looked around me as I shifted, vaguely aware that I'd landed in the middle of the drawbridge. I was sure the townsfolk didn't appreciate the sudden sight of their naked king, but I didn't care.

We had to move fast. A shiver ran up my spine. I had failed to protect Stavrok's beloved cousin.

He'll have my head on a spike.

I would deserve it. Hell, I'd *support* it.

The realization flooded over me then and there.

I loved Cass. I needed her by my side. And I was going to do whatever it took to bring her back to me.

Jace strode up to me, expression clouded with worry. He held out a robe and I dragged it over my shoulders, falling into step beside him as we entered the castle.

"Gather the men," I instructed my commander, Eric, who snapped to attention at once. All around me, people whispered to each other, hushed and frantic. "There's no time to waste."

"Sire?" Jace put a broad hand on my shoulder. It was a familiar gesture, and one I appreciated. Right now, I needed people I could trust, not servants bowing before their king. "What happened?"

"Cass, she…" The words lodged in my throat and I swallowed hard, jaw tightening. The very mention of her name sent my shifter reeling. "They've taken her."

Keeping my voice low, I told him about the dragon shifters I'd fought in the woods, the hordes of wolves, trained like attack dogs to take down anything in their path.

Jace's eyes darkened. "Raiders."

There it was. The word that had haunted our kingdom for years. The dark figures that still filled my people's nightmares, filling their thoughts with smoke, death, and ruin.

"Yes." I bowed my head. Although we were speaking quietly, I glanced around, making sure no-one could overhear us. "In the woods, by the mountains. I'm not sure how many."

"Thought we'd wiped most of them out." Jace frowned, running a hand over his thick beard. "I guess scavengers find a way to survive. You sure we have the strength to face them, Sire?"

I stared at the ground, gathering the strength to say what needed to be said.

In truth, I didn't know if we would survive this, but I wasn't going to stop until Cass was safe again.

Eventually I lifted my head and looked him right in the eye. "We leave at sunset."

Jace simply nodded. He trusted me. I wouldn't send my men into a fight they had no hope of winning.

As I watched him walk away, I knew what I had to do.

～

Cass

I had no option but to follow the guy who'd come into my hut.

We bypassed the firepit, circling around it and heading toward the largest hut in the small encampment.

For whatever reason, they hadn't blindfolded me. Small faces peered at me as I passed, with people coming and going out of the thick forest around us. They were fetching firewood and mending things. The wolves were nowhere to be seen.

My guard came to a standstill at the doorway of the hut. He gestured silently toward the door. I hesitated, terrified to discover what was on the other side.

The guard gave me a nudge. It wasn't a harsh one, but it told me I didn't have a choice in the matter.

Reluctantly, I walked through the door.

The hut was dim inside, although a small fire burned under a bubbling pot. Two men sat on low seats just behind it. They stood up when I came in, and my hackles rose.

"Where am I?" I asked, trying not to let fear bleed into my voice.

Then, I remembered something. The guard had called me *Your Highness.* I definitely wasn't some random girl to them.

"You know who I am." I crept forward. They regarded me impassively, still mostly in shadow. "Why have you done this?"

"Princess Cassandra," the one on the left said. His voice was rough, unused. It reminded me of woodsmoke, or the logs crackling over the firepit. "Welcome to our camp."

He moved a fraction closer. As his face caught the light, I froze with shock.

His face was strikingly familiar to the man who had just broken my heart. He had the same high cheekbones, the same piercing, ice-blue eyes.

His face was broader, however, and his hair longer and wilder. He had a fair amount of stubble, and a scar at the edge of his jaw. His bare arms told me he'd seen his share of combat.

"Who are you?" I whispered.

I wanted to be afraid, but some part of me whispered that I wasn't in danger. My dragon slumbered in my chest, unphased by the unfolding action.

"He's Dymitri," the man on the right said. He had a smoother voice, a deep, rich baritone, and when the flames fell across his face, he too bore a striking resemblance to Damon. "And I'm Lucian."

"This is your camp."

"Yes." Dymitri crouched before the fire, drawing out a cup and filling it with something that smelled delicious. "Please, eat. You must be hungry."

I was, but I took the cup from him without bringing it to my lips. I had no reason to trust these people.

I pressed my mouth together, considering the two of them. "You shot me out of the sky and dragged me here and flung me in a prison room."

Dymitri looked downcast. "We're deeply sorry. You have to understand… my brother and I wish you no harm, Princess."

I wrinkled my nose and corrected them. "Just Cassandra."

Dymitri nodded. Wordlessly, he swept out an arm, indicating a cushion by the fireside. I sank down onto it, curling my hands around my cup, letting it warm me.

"We seek an audience with the new king." Lucian returned to his seat. He was less forthcoming than his brother, seemingly content to stare into the flames. "We needed a bargaining tool."

"And I just happened to fall out of the sky," I said dryly, mouth twisting. "Quite literally."

"Please." Dymitri shot a glare at Lucian, who merely raised an eyebrow. He leaned forward, catching my gaze. "Our people are desperate. Survival out here is… perilous, to say the least."

Lucian snorted but didn't comment.

Pieces of the puzzle were falling into place in my mind.

"Those raiders who burned and ransacked the kingdom…" I stared into the flames, frowning as if the answers lay there. "That wasn't you, was it?"

"No." Dymitri pressed a hand against his forearm, thumb tracing over a white, raised scar. "We've run into them ourselves on many occasions. When they were defeated, that's when word got back to us that the old king was dead."

Lucian smiled, but it didn't reach his eyes. "We've spent our lives in exile, along with our entire village."

"Why?"

As we talked, the wild men of my imagination transformed, growing less and less fearsome the longer I looked at them. I began to see them as they truly were: two young men who were just as scared as I was.

"The old king didn't take kindly to reminders that he was less than a perfect husband; a perfect father." Dymitri exchanged a grim look with his brother. "We were living proof."

"You're his sons." As I said it, I knew it was true. I'd known it from the moment I saw them. "Damon's brothers."

"Half-brothers," Lucian said. "But yes."

"We want to talk with King Damon." Dymitri folded his hands together, looking at me intently. "But we knew we had to be careful. Nobody here knows him; knows what kind of man he is. If he's like his father…"

"He isn't," I interjected. "He… he cares about his people. He wants to rebuild his kingdom. That's his main priority."

I could hardly think of Damon without ice flooding into my heart, but I wouldn't lie about him. He may have rejected me as his mate, but I *could* say that much for him. He only wanted to recover what his father had lost. Nothing mattered more to him than that.

Not even me.

Something of my anguish must have shown on my face. If the brothers noticed, they didn't say anything, much to my relief.

"We have no interest in challenging his rule." Lucian turned to me. "We just want to live in peace."

They both stared at me for a lengthy moment. I narrowed my eyes at them, and then turned my attention to the delicious broth in my cup. I took a big sip, savoring the flavor.

Finally, I set down the cup and turned to face them fully.

"You two…" I stared between them. "Are *idiots*."

Their eyes widened in shock, but I wasn't done.

I've been blasted with dragon ice fire, dragged through the woods, and held hostage. I am going to say my piece, and they're gonna listen!

"You should have come and talked to him! Like rational people! Damon is *good*. He won't turn you away, or hurt you, or whatever it is you're so afraid of! He's a good man, and he needs good, strong men to help him rebuild the kingdom." I drew a shuddering breath. "And if you take me back with you, *I* can smooth over this huge misunderstanding, and we can all move on with our lives."

I crossed my arms over my chest and glowered at them.

Dymitri and Lucian gaped at me.

I raised one eyebrow, and then the other crept up to join it.

"Got it," Dymitri said eventually.

I exhaled.

"Good!" I kicked out my legs, stretching them before the fire. I was warmed through now, and relaxed. Finally. "By the way, Damon won't take kindly to the whole kidnapping thing, so you might want to let *me* do the talking to start with."

By the looks on their faces, it was clear they hadn't considered the ramifications of holding me hostage.

I gave them a cheery smile. "Can I have some more broth now?"

An hour later, we were ready to go.

Lucian disappeared outside to tell the others that the camp was on the move.

Dymitri and I stayed by the fire, trading stories. He had never been south of the mountains, and he wanted to know everything about what it was like to grow up in green, peaceful valleys, where life wasn't a continuous struggle for survival.

In return, he told me more about the kingdom of the north.

"Damon's father was happy, once." He twirled the stick in his hand, which he had been using to poke at the fire, as he considered his words. "His mother... she wasn't born here, in the north. Did you know that?"

I shook my head. Curiosity burned in my chest.

"Damon's father saw her one day, when he was visiting the southern kingdoms to sign a trade deal. He carried her off."

Dymitri glanced at me, and I nodded. I knew how these things typically went, after all. Stavrok was a prime example, except Lucy had been in a human village when he'd carried her off.

"She was adored by the people... and by the king. But when she died, it was whispered that the ice and snow killed her. She wasn't made for the north. She didn't belong here...." His head dropped. "Forgive me, Cassandra. I don't mean to suggest that you..."

"It's okay," I was quick to reassure him. "I know."

Well, that definitely explains a lot about Damon's fears for my safety...

"Come on," Dymitri said eventually, clambering to his feet and offering a hand. "We should be ready to leave soon."

We emerged from the tent.

"That was fast!" I said, startled.

The camp site had been completely dismantled. All that remained of the fire pit was a smoldering pile of ash. A huddle of caravans, laden with belongings, waited for us at the edge of the tree line.

Dymitri gave a loose shrug. "We're used to packing up in a hurry, I guess."

A wolf prowled the edge of the forest, and fear trickled down my spine as a small girl rushed up to it and buried her hands deep in its thick pelt.

The wolf lowered its head and let the girl pet it. It was strange to see such a large, ferocious beast act so gentle.

Maybe I've misjudged this place.

"Ready when you are, Cassandra," Lucian shouted. He held the reins of a sturdy-looking horse. "Your carriage awaits."

I smiled at him.

The sky above us went dark. Several people screamed as they stared into the clouds.

I glanced upwards, and my eyes widened as I made out the shadow of wings, so vast they blocked out the sun.

A jet of silver fire burst across the sky, and my heart stopped.

"No!" I screamed, waving my hands frantically. For a heartbeat, I considered shifting, but by then it would be too late.

I could only watch as Damon circled the clearing above us.

CHAPTER 14

Cass

Dymitri and Lucian rushed forward, and fresh panic gripped me as their dragons gleamed in their eyes. They were about to shift, and he'd kill them both.

"He wants me!" I ran toward them, and they stopped in their tracks. "He won't hurt you. He's just looking for me!"

I had no idea how true that was, but I had to believe Damon wouldn't attack an entire camp just to get to me.

The sky lit up again with icy flames.

Dymitri wheeled to face me. "Are you sure about that?"

I closed my eyes, reaching out with every ounce of mental strength I had in me. My soul searched for its mate, up into the cloud bank above our heads. A flash of coldness ran through me, a fury unlike anything I'd felt before.

Damon.

It was his rage I felt. His anger, his terror.

Damon... Damon, I'm here. I'm safe. Please...

I let out a gasp, and my eyes opened.

The huge dragon descended into the clearing, its clawed feet leaving deep gouge marks in the earth. He roared, and the deep, powerful sound shook the earth under our feet.

Damon's dragon was huge. Bigger than I could've imagined, with a wingspan that easily stretched across the whole camp.

His hide was pale, shimmering silver in the dim light. His eyes were the same icy blue as they were in his human form. The spikes that covered his head were sharp and deadly. As he lowered his head, they reminded me of a crown.

He was magnificent.

I stepped forward, separating myself from the group. I spared a glance behind me and kept my voice quiet but firm as I instructed a woman nearby. "Bring me a robe for the king."

She hurried off.

I turned and faced him. His eyes were already fixed on me. Even from this distance I could see his huge chest rise and fall with barely suppressed fury.

"I'm here," I said. "I'm unhurt, look."

The woman scuttled up behind me and I took the robe from her with a nod.

I sensed the tension in the clearing. At any moment, it could break.

It's all up to me.

All my life I'd been told what to do. By my courtiers, my own family. None of that mattered any more. I wasn't about to hide from Damon and let him destroy these innocents in my name.

I moved closer, positioning myself between the dragon and the frightened villagers. I knew that Damon wouldn't harm them if there was a chance that he'd hurt me in the process.

As I got within range, he moved sharply, as if to grab me. I stepped back and glared at him, shaking my head. He huffed with annoyance and glowered at me but lowered his head.

I tilted up my chin at him, triumphant.

I'm not going to be carried back to the castle like a sack of potatoes.

I raised an eyebrow at him, and watched the fire in his gaze flicker, smoldering into embers. A hazy mist built up as he shifted, and when it cleared, Damon stood in the middle of the clearing.

Even unclothed, his human form was imposing. His gaze was fixed directly on me, but his sheer presence was enough to freeze everyone to the spot.

I stepped forward with the robe held between my two hands.

He looked at me, his burning gaze unreadable.

Then, he fell to his knees and bowed his head—to my shock, and likely the shock of everyone else in the clearing.

I knew what I had to do. Gently, I lay the robe over his shoulders. It was a coronation of sorts. The movement felt ceremonial, regal. When he rose to his feet, he drew the robe around to cover himself and took my hand.

"My king," I murmured.

He bent and kissed my fingers.

The gesture was formal, more for the benefit of those watching than anything else. Nevertheless, when his mouth brushed against my skin a tremor ran through my body.

He dropped my hand, and his gaze moved past me, onto the crowd at the edge of the trees.

"Who is in charge here?"

"We are." Dymitri's voice rang out across the clearing.

Lucian stood by his side, unspeaking and unsmiling. Tension was written into every muscle in their bodies.

Damon narrowed his eyes, but the expression mingled with surprise, which morphed into open astonishment.

He'd picked up on the likeness between them.

Good. That will hopefully make this easier.

I gripped Damon's arm tight, and his gaze flicked down to meet mine.

"Come on." I smiled up at him. "Let's go meet your brothers."

"Brothers?" he whispered, seemingly to himself. We moved together, crossing the ground at a slow, careful pace. Damon looked like he was in a dream.

Finally, we drew level with them.

"Your Majesty," I said, looping my arm through his, so he didn't swing out at them. "Allow me to introduce Dymitri and Lucian."

Damon regarded the two men, who both inclined their heads at him in an identical fashion.

"Cass tells me we're brothers." Damon's voice was low, and still held an edge of danger. "I'll admit that I can see it. That's the only reason I haven't reduced this entire clearing to ash."

Lucian's lip curled, and Dymitri flashed him a glare of warning.

"King Damon," he said. "Our mother was the daughter of our village's blacksmith. The old king sent us into exile after the queen's death… along with half the village, as you can see."

As he spoke, Damon sidled closer to me, tucking me in against his side. Shielding me.

Internally, I sighed.

Is stubbornness a genetic trait amongst these ice dragons?

"Damon," I interjected, pulling away slightly. "They were never going to hurt me. They needed some way to get your attention, and I was just in the wrong place at the wrong time."

"My attention?" Damon's eyes flashed, although thankfully there was no trace of the dragon behind his gaze. "Why?"

"We wish to come back, Your Majesty," Lucian said. Although his face was as somber as ever, his tone was sincere. "We were banished from the kingdom many years ago, but now that our father is dead, we hoped you might let us return."

"The old king threatened our lives," Dymitri added. "We had no idea what kind of man you were. We needed… leverage."

"Then you got more than you bargained for," Damon said fiercely. "Cass is *not* a bargaining chip."

"Damon." I placed a soothing hand on his shoulder, and he relaxed beneath my touch. "They know. They only want to talk. That's all. Look at them. They want to be safe again. These people deserve protection. Your brothers deserve protection."

Damon stared down at me. Then, he took my face in his hands and pressed a gentle kiss to my forehead.

"Of course," he murmured. "Thank you, Cass."

Our argument earlier felt like a distant dream. I tried to recall my anger, how furious I'd been, but seeing him like this now, I could feel only love.

He had listened to me. Actually *listened.*

Relief flooded Dymitri and Lucian's faces, and all those behind them began to relax and chatter amongst themselves in low, excited voices. I couldn't help but feel a spark of pride.

Damon straightened up, looking over the entire gathering, although his gaze soon returned to his brothers.

"You are all welcome to return. The kingdom is your home, and its gates will always be open to you." He lowered his voice, addressing Dymitri and Lucian directly. "Come to live with us in the castle. For as long as you want. God knows we've got the space." The use of the word *we* lifted my heart, but I couldn't question it right now.

There was too much going on to worry about whether Damon meant what he said, or if I'd got the wrong end of the stick from him yet again.

DAMON

I waited until the last of the caravans trundled out of the clearing before turning to Cass.

We stood in the middle of the empty space, surrounded by bare patches of earth, where tents had been pitched.

Cass refused to meet my gaze.

"Cass, please." I reached out a hand, and then pulled it back, uncertain. "Allow me to explain myself."

She tucked her arms around her body, biting her lip. The dark fringe of her lashes hid her eyes from me. "What is there to explain?"

"When I first saw you, I…" Unable to help it, I rushed forward, but I didn't dare touch her yet. "You know how I felt. How we felt. It terrified me. I couldn't see anything beyond your youth, your inexperience. You were this delicate, beautiful woman who had stumbled into a harsh wilderness… I knew there was no way you could survive it.

And I had trapped you here. I hated myself for putting you in that position."

"Thanks," Cass said tonelessly. Her eyes were flat and dull, all traces of their usual spark snuffed out.

"I was wrong."

Cass looked up sharply. "What?"

I drew a deep, shuddering breath, and lay a hand on her shoulder. "I was wrong, Cass. And you were right. I was so wrapped up in the past, my father's mistakes, that I couldn't see what was right in front of me. When I watched you drop out of the sky—" I broke off, shaking my head against the memory. "I've never been so afraid in my life. And I realized, I can't keep focusing on the what-ifs anymore."

"What are you saying?" Cass whispered.

"I've been so caught up with wanting you gone..." I leaned forward, forcing her to meet my eye. "I wanted what I thought was best for you, for us. I wasn't seeing you for who you are. You're brave, smart..."

"Keep talking." The corners of her mouth curled upwards, and some of the light crept back into her eyes.

"You brought me back to life, Cass." There it was. The truth I had been running from all this time. "I can't live without you. I know that now. I'd give up my kingdom, I'd give the whole world, just to keep you by my side."

"I'm stronger than you think," she said, as her hand came up and clutched mine, squeezing my fingers gently. Emboldened by the gesture, I reached up and brushed her hair off her face, running my fingers through her curls. "I still want to stay, Damon."

My heart swelled, and I pressed a kiss against her mouth. She returned it eagerly, and for a moment we stood there in the clearing, tangled up in each other.

"Then stay," I breathed, watching her cheeks flush. "Stay and be my queen."

"Is this a proposal?"

Despite everything that had passed between us, the nerves still crowded my stomach.

"It is." I bowed my head, before falling to my knees and taking her small hands in mine. "All that I have is yours. It's not… all you're used to."

I looked up at her. She was gazing down at me, her expression soft.

"Maybe," Cass whispered, "but it's all I need."

I reached into my shirt and drew out my thin silver chain, fingering the ring on the end. Cass's eyes widened, and she watched in rapt focus as I undid the chain and held the ring up to the light.

"This belonged to my mother." I turned the ring over in my fingers, memories crowding my mind. "My father gave it to her not long after they met."

It was small, silver-wrought, and delicate. Roses crept along the band, entwined with thorns.

"It's beautiful," Cass said.

I held it out to her.

"It's too small for me to wear," I said. "So, I kept it on a chain."

Close to my heart.

"Ever since she…" I swallowed, not being able to say the words. But from the look on her face, she caught my meaning. "I want you to have it, Cass. *She* would want you to have it."

Cass fiddled with the ring. Gently, I took it back from her and slid it onto her finger. It fit her perfectly.

"Roses and thorns." She chuckled to herself.

"Beauty and harshness." I straightened and stood up. As I drew my arms tightly around her waist, she leaned into my body. "In this land, you'll have to get used to both, I'm afraid."

"Well, then, I guess I'll need some warmer clothing," she said, and stood on her tiptoes, lifting her face.

I tilted my head down, and readily gave her the kiss she wordlessly asked for.

As I knew I always would.

EPILOGUE

Cass

I gasped as a dish was set down in front of us by a servant, and the cover removed with a flourish. Beside me, Damon's eyes danced with amusement.

"Strawberries!" I shouted, loud enough for several guests' heads to swivel around. "You remembered!"

Undeterred by the eyes on me, I reached forward and shoved a strawberry into my mouth, groaning as the sweetness burst across my tongue.

Damon chuckled, watching me. He accepted the strawberry I pressed into his hand and raised an eyebrow as he bit into it, clearly surprised by the sweet taste.

"Good, right?" I grinned.

He nodded. He was humoring me to some degree, but I didn't care.

I snuggled in against his side, humming with contentment. I turned my face up to him. "I can't believe you remembered what I said!"

"Of course, love." He trailed a finger over the back of my hand. I turned my palm up and let him lace our fingers together. "Anything for you."

The hall was packed with well-wishers and admirers. It was hard to believe that a few short months ago, this place was so dark and still. Now, the carved wooden paneling gleamed, and the high arched windows framed the snow drifting down outside.

Granted, it was a little different to the celebrations I was used to. The decorations around the hall mixed the north and south together, symbolizing our union; delicate sprigs of blossom and pink ribbons were dotted around the tables, and shiny glass icicles hung from the high ceiling, sparkling in the sunlight.

It shouldn't work, but it did. I smiled, catching sight of the banner hanging on the far wall. Wolves and dragons interwoven together, and the whole thing entwined with a border of roses.

Summer and winter.

I wasn't stupid. I knew that life would never be the same again. That there would be challenges thrown our way. But I didn't care. Besides, who *didn't* have challenges?

I'd chosen my destiny. Where others might see danger lurking around every corner of this land, I only saw adventure.

Not to mention the man I love.

Along the top table, we sat with our friends and fellow rulers. The smaller round tables filled the rest of the space in the Great Hall. I caught sight of Rob, who I'd learnt knew everything there was to know about the history of the kingdom. At another table sat Dymitri and Lucian. They had declined the offer to sit beside us, but seemed content enough to observe the proceedings, if slightly unnerved by the number of people.

I let my eyes wander, smiling every time I spotted a familiar face. More and more of them *were* familiar, these days. The change in their king had won over most of the townsfolk, and every day it got easier to chat to them.

They weren't really as cold as people said. You just needed to get to know them.

And I had all the time in the world for that.

"It's time," Damon murmured, and I straightened up in excitement, squeezing his hand as he got up from the table.

As his chair scraped backwards, I locked eyes with Marienne who sat a table away. She waggled her fingers at me playfully. Damon headed across the floor, weaving his way through the tables, and as I watched him go, Marienne chuckled to herself.

"What?"

Marienne raised her glass of tonic water with one hand and cradled her round belly with the other.

"Nothing, nothing." A smug smile was playing around her mouth. "I'm pleased you've found your happiness here, Cass."

Rage leaned over and draped an arm over her shoulder. "My wife is the matchmaker of the kingdom." He smirked. "I think it's gone to her head."

He sounded a little annoyed, but the way he looked at her said otherwise. Pride shone in his eyes.

"Not at all." Marienne stuck out her tongue at him, and he laughed. "It's just nice to use my powers for something good, for a change."

Rage's eyes softened, and something unspoken passed between them. I turned my head away to give them their privacy, scanning the crowd for Damon.

My husband!

I still couldn't believe it. I was a married woman now, a queen.

A broad hand fell on my shoulder, and I looked up to be confronted with the full force of Stavrok's broad, beaming smile.

"Cass." He hauled me up out of my seat.

I wheezed as he pulled me into a bone-crushing hug.

"Oof!" I pulled away from him a little, laughing. "Stavrok!"

Stavrok gazed down at me, misty-eyed. "I'm so proud of you, Cass."

"Looks like I figured things out on my own, huh?" I tilted my head, unable to resist teasing him a little. "No rescues necessary."

"Look at you." He glanced around at the bright hallway, and the snowy landscape outside. "You're the Queen of Winter."

I let out a chuckle. Lucy appeared at Stavrok's side, flushed and happy, her long fair hair braided up at the top of her head. It had been some months since I'd seen her, and I gasped at the bump under her dress.

"He's all smiles now, isn't he?" She looped an easy arm around Stavrok's waist. "Be glad you didn't have to see me wrestle him into his tux this morning."

"Lucy!"

Lucy let me pull her into a tight hug, giggling as I squealed and hopped up and down with excitement. "Oh, my God! Why didn't you tell me you were expecting?"

I drew back. I couldn't punch her in the shoulder, so I punched Stavrok instead, who glared and rubbed his arm.

"Jeez, Cass! You're lucky it's your wedding day."

Lucy looked unconcerned with her husband's plight. Her eyes danced with happiness. "I wanted it to be a surprise!"

"Hang on…" I glanced over at Marienne, who was deep in conversation with Rage, still cradling her own pregnant belly. "Did you do this on purpose?"

Lucy just shrugged, but a smirk appeared at the corner of her mouth. "What? They'll all grow up together! It'll be so cute."

Stavrok shot me a look that said, *don't even ask.*

Not that I wanted to. The less I knew about their sex life, the better, given some of the things I'd had the misfortune to hear back when I lived with them.

Luckily, Damon chose that moment to reappear out of the crowd, his two half-brothers in tow.

They were both dressed in suits in honor of the day. They felt as uncomfortable as Stavrok did in the fine garments, judging by the way they kept tugging at their collars. They looked good, strong and regal. A far cry from the rough-hewn shifter men I'd met in the woods, all those weeks ago.

Although Damon and his newfound brothers had warmed to each other considerably since their first meeting, Dymitri looked apprehensive, his pale eyes narrow and his brow furrowed. Lucian looked downright suspicious as they reached the foot of the table.

"What is this?" Dymitri asked.

"You'll see," Damon said with a wink.

I grinned back at him. I'd been looking forward to this moment.

"Marienne, would you mind?" I turned back to Dymitri. "Marienne has a very special gift. She's agreed to use it on the two of you."

"My wedding present." Marienne stepped up from the table. "To Cass and Damon."

Dymitri still looked unsure. "That's very generous of you, Damon, but it's not necessary…"

Damon held up a hand. "After everything the two of you suffered at the hands of our father, I want to give you a gift. Something you'll treasure forever. It's the least I can do."

As he slid back into his seat, I turned to him and gave him a big smile.

"What?"

"Nothing!" My smile grew bigger. "I'm just happy."

He let out a huff, but I could tell he was pleased. My head dropped into the crook of his neck and his arm came up around my shoulder, his fingers tracing lazy patterns against the back of my neck.

"Have I told you how gorgeous you look right now?" he murmured.

"Yes." I glanced up at him. "Many times, actually."

Whatever his reply was, I found myself distracted by a sudden purple haze of light that erupted over the floor before us, flowing out from Marienne's outstretched hands.

Several onlookers gasped, but the crowd wasn't fearful. Most of our guests knew Marienne, and watched, fascinated, as the shimmering smoke continued to spiral outwards. Lucy had told me all about Marienne's courage, how she'd risked her life fighting in the battle. It was clear that she was a heroine in the eyes of these people. I was glad her powers were a source of admiration to them, rather than fear.

With a deep, shuddering breath, she collapsed to her knees, utterly spent. In a flash, Rage was by her side, stroking a hand over her back. When she looked up, however, her eyes were wide with excitement.

"I know where they are!"

As she spoke, her eyes wandered over to… Lucy, of all people.

"Where?" I asked. Why was she looking at Lucy?

"Not here, that's for sure." Marienne got to her feet, still trembling a little. She was fast regaining her strength, stronger than she had been the last time we met. "They're beyond the portal. In the human realm."

"Who are?" Dymitri asked. "What are you talking about? What's going on?"

Lucian said nothing, but he looked equally impatient to know the answer.

Marienne blinked, like she'd forgotten about them altogether. She glanced at Damon. "You… didn't tell them?"

"Tell us *what?*" Dymitri demanded.

"Damon asked me to find them for you. Like I did for him and Cass. And Stavrok and Lucy. I used my magic to find the women you're fated to be with," Marienne said. Her shoulders rose and fell as she shrugged, and the sleeves of her elegant gown fluttered around her. Her eyes were wide. "They're in danger."

My stomach twisted. "What do you mean?"

Marienne swayed against Rage, who put an arm around her waist and drew her into his side. She pressed a hand to her temple, like the memory pained her.

"I saw… an old house. A farmhouse. A pickup truck. And…" She looked up, her long dark hair falling over her face. She'd gone pale. "A locked door. The women are together, but they're—they're trapped."

"Hold on a second," Lucian demanded. "Are you saying our soul-mates are human?"

"Yes," Marienne snapped. "There's no time for the finer details. You have to hurry."

Dymitri was already tugging loose his tie, unbuttoning his shirt like he was getting ready to shift then and there. The entire hall was hushed, agog. Dymitri and Lucian's gazes flicked back and forth between Marienne and the others like they were watching a tennis match.

Lucian's hand shot out and he grabbed his brother's wrist. "Wait. Where exactly are these women?"

Marienne strode forward. Instead of replying, she simply pressed two fingers against Lucian's forehead. His eyes slid shut and when he opened them, his astonishment chased away the last remaining shreds of doubt and confusion.

"Thank you," he said, and she nodded, satisfied.

Marienne turned toward the table, where the rest of us were still looking on in shock.

"I've just given them directions. They know how to get there..." She paused, looking worried. "In theory, anyway."

Stavrok stood so fast that the silverware and glasses clattered over the table. "I'll go with them. They'll need a guide, someone who understands the human realm. And human women, come to that."

He glanced down at Lucy, who patted him on the arm.

"My husband isn't the type to back down from a fight," Lucy added darkly. "Promise me you'll come back in one piece?"

Stavrok bent to kiss the top of her head. "Always. You know I'd take you with me, but..." His gaze fell pointedly on her belly. "I won't be gone long, love."

He was already shrugging out of his jacket, the light of his dragon surging in his eyes. Damon sauntered up beside me. I took his hand in mine, and together we watched Stavrok stride out of the hall, Dymitri and Lucian hot on his heels.

"Well, that was exciting," I said.

Damon's mouth quirked. "Did you expect anything else?"

I laughed and shook my head. Soon it would be time to cut the cake, and after that there would be dancing, and the snow-covered grounds would be full of people, music, and laughter.

And after that? I fiddled with the silver ring around my finger, smiling. It had company now, my wedding band.

There were many more adventures to come.

THE END

AFTERWORD

Book 4 in the Fire and Ice series will be out later this year!

But if you have enjoyed this steamy shifter romance, then you will LOVE my Halloween Witches series.
Book 1- Alpha Magic is available now.
You can buy it or download it : HERE

Or read on for a sneak peek here:

PROLOGUE

*H*alloween night. One year ago.

RUBY

Our mothers said that three of us were Fated, blessed. What she meant was, I would be stuck with these two pain-in-the-ass best friends until my dying day.

"So, are we going to do this, or not?" I asked my friends, staring at each of them in turn. "Because there's no going back after this."

My heart was pounding like a runaway train and if we didn't cast the spell now, I was afraid we'd never have the guts to do it.

The wind moved through the trees around us, rustling the leaves and signaling a Fall storm was on its way. We were gathered outside beneath the full moon and dark, starless sky, on a large piece of property in the middle of nowhere.

No one could see us, and as long as we never said a word, nobody would ever know about our little adventure on this night.

This Halloween night. Our joint twenty-first birthday.

Tiffany, the blonde bombshell of our little group, nodded fiercely. I could see the determination in her bright blue eyes. She wanted this as much I did.

I turned to Bella, who had her teeth buried firmly in her lower lip.

I rolled my eyes. "Come on, Bella. You know we can't do this without you."

And I meant that literally. Bella was a powerful witch and without her magic, I wasn't sure Tiff and I could pull off a spell of this magnitude.

She frowned and I could see the hesitation in the set of her shoulders, in her dark brown gaze.

I narrowed my eyes at the girl who'd been practically a sister to me since the day we'd been born. "Come on, Bella. Please."

We'd been talking about this spell for years, planning every part of the complex incantation. Waiting until the night we were old enough… powerful enough… gutsy enough, to pull it off.

Suddenly Bella's gaze hardened, and relief poured through me. I knew that look. She was on my side now.

"Okay, Ruby. I'm in. Let's do this."

I grabbed my two best friends' hands and they grabbed each other, forming a perfect triangle of strength.

We were three witches born on the same day, the most powerful day of the year for our kind. All Hallows' Eve.

Our mothers were best friends, united in the abandonment by the fathers of their children. They'd made sure we grew up together, strong, bonded, and most of all, loyal to one another.

We clasped hands and glanced down at the book between us, a spell book I'd found ten years ago, hidden in my mother's things. A powerful spell book that had belonged to my late grandmother.

We began to chant in an ancient language that no one used anymore.

I closed my eyes, having memorized the spell years ago. I spoke my part and my friends spoke theirs. Each section was a call to the magic that rippled in our veins. To Fate. And most of all, to the unconditional love that we all desired and craved.

Over and over we chanted our words, the magic in our blood, in our ancestry, simmering and bursting at the seams.

I could feel the heat in my body building until sweat rolled down my face. I didn't stop, and neither did Bella or Tiffany. The power of our combined words swirled around us like a hurricane, and I clung to the spell, focusing everything I had on this night. This one moment, where we would make sure that we'd never end up like our mothers, abandoned and alone.

My eyes opened. The ancient book floated in the air between us. Bella was watching the book with trepidation and Tiff grinned when she caught my eye.

We began to speak louder, the words in our hearts building naturally as the spell came to a crescendo. I stared at our joined hands as white light built between our clenched fingers.

There was a sudden surge of power, and the urge to finish the spell gripped me. I nodded at my honorary sisters and together we spoke the last of our parts. There was no going back now.

As we uttered those last few words, the white magic we'd conjured shot into the air above our heads, exploding into a spectacular spray of fireworks highlighted against the dark night sky.

The impact of the explosion blew us back and apart, each of us landing with a thump on the grass.

I groaned as I rolled onto my side to take pressure off the bruised parts of my backside but I didn't look away from the sky as the magic exploded, then seemed to disappear.

A small amount of disappointment hit me. I'd expected more than some white fireworks, then dissipation. Though what I'd thought would happen, I didn't know.

As we sat on the ground surrounded by nature and trees and the gorgeous country house off in the distance, peace stole over me.

"Is that it?" I asked, and as though in answer, the spell book that had been hovering in the air between us, landed in the dirt. The front cover closed, all signs of magic, gone.

Tiffany stood first, brushing the dirt from her tight pants and groaning as though annoyed by the mess.

Bella and I got to our feet too, the excitement and build-up to this day beginning to leach the strength out of me.

It was over. It was done. Now, all we had to do was wait for the spell to come to fruition. For the men—our men—to come to us.

And patience, although I'd been told was a virtue, was not one of my strengths.

"So… back to the house for a celebratory drink?" I suggested, forcing some excitement into my tone.

We'd brought some alcohol with us. Why wouldn't we, when we could finally legally drink in the human world?

"Sounds like a plan," Tiffany said with a flick of her long hair, and together we turned and trekked back to the house that Bella's family owned.

I glanced down at my hands, expecting something to have changed. But as I glanced at each of my friends, it seemed that nothing was different for any of us. Not physically, anyway.

I wondered if our loves, wherever they were, had been hit with our magic. Could they feel it, even now? Were they searching for us?

Once inside the little house in the woods, we flicked on the lights and used our magic to mix up cocktails the color of the sunset—red, yellow, and a splash of purple.

"Perfect." I picked up my glass that had been resting on the counter.

Tiffany and Bella plucked up their drinks as well, raising their glasses to clink with mine.

"Happy birthday," I said, and they chorused back to me.

Sharing a birthday with my two best friends had been trying at times, especially growing up. I'd never had my own party, or a single day when I could feel simply special just for being me.

But now, I loved it.

We all took a sip of our first legal drink and grimaced at the amount of liquor I'd poured in.

"Wow, that's strong," Tiff said, blinking rapidly.

I nodded, swallowing hard as the vodka and gin mix slid down my throat.

Bella gulped awkwardly, shuddering before she set the drink back down on the counter. She waved her hand over the table in front of us and conjured up a whole feast of savory and sweet snacks. Chips, chocolate cake, cookies, and crackers with cheese littered the surface in front of us.

She was the best at making food. Actually, she was the best of everything when it came to magic. But luckily for us, as the most introverted of our trio, she never threw it in our faces.

"Oh, perfect. Thanks, Belle."

I grabbed some chips and stuffed them in my mouth. I hadn't eaten dinner with all the nerves surrounding tonight.

Bella sighed and I glanced up at her, raising my eyebrows in question. It was obvious she wanted to ask me something.

"What's up Bell-Bell?"

"Do you think it worked?" she asked, speaking aloud the question we all wanted answered.

I shrugged, forcing myself to appear nonchalant, though I was anything but. This spell would hopefully change the course of all our lives for the better.

I gave her the only answer I could. "I don't know. I hope so."

"So do I!" Tiffany said, her tone exasperated. "We've only been planning this forever."

I conjured up some stools and we all sat down around our little birthday feast.

We chatted and ate, drank and laughed, celebrating our whole lives ahead of us.

Through the night I hoped that our magic was working its way to the men for whom we were destined, because the spell we had woven together tonight was a spell that called out to destiny. For our one, true love.

All three of our mothers had been abandoned before we were even born. We'd grown up around sorrow and loneliness. Heartache.

None of us wanted that for ourselves or any future children we might have.

So tonight, we'd sent out a call for the men who would love us for all eternity. Our perfect matches. Men who would stand by us. Love us. Never leave us.

We wanted them quickly of course, but they would answer the call when they were good and ready. Or at least, that was what I assumed.

Whether that be tomorrow, next month, or next year, I would wait. And I knew Bella and Tiffany would, too.

Because only Fate could be trusted with such an important a decision as the person we were meant to spend the rest of our lives with.

Born to three single mothers, not a father between us, we had trust issues aplenty. I, for one, wasn't going to just date anyone.

And I certainly wasn't going to fall in love with the first guy who happened to look my way. I'd rather be alone forever than live with the pain my mother wore like a heavy coat.

So hopefully, Fate and our own magic would not let us down, because we'd risked everything tonight to make our futures happen.

CHAPTER 1

One year later.

Ruby

My day job at the local florist certainly wasn't glamorous, but it passed the time all the same.

"Have a nice day," I said to the human woman who'd bought a bunch of roses for her sick mother. I waved her out the door. What I really should have done was tuck in a spell for her mother's flu, but we weren't allowed to do magic around the humans in town.

I let out a huge sigh and looked around the large shop filled with buckets of brightly colored flowers and potted plants. What was I doing here again?

Making yourself useful until you work out what you want to do with your life, my mother's voice sounded in my head.

The witches in my family were healers, fortune tellers, teachers. But unlike all those women who had come before me, I had no idea what I wanted to do with my life at this point.

I'd graduated high school with good grades, gone to community college, then… nothing.

I was adrift, and that wasn't my personality generally. I wasn't a flake. But unlike so many of the witching community who were addicted to the coven lifestyle, I just… wasn't.

I wasn't even sure if I wanted to hang around this town forever. Travel sounded more interesting to me, seeing the world. If only I could convince Bella and Tiffany to come.

"Ruby, I'm just heading to the bank. Do you want me to grab anything for your lunch?" Andrea, my boss, smiled at me as she picked up her handbag from behind the counter and headed to the front door.

"No. I'm all good today. Thanks, Andrea." I waved at her as she left.

Such a lovely woman, especially for a human.

When my mother had realized I couldn't make up my mind on what I wanted to do with my life, she'd forced me to get a job with a non-magical person. To learn, to expand my horizons. To be "of use to the community".

Which, at the time, I'd thought was a horrible idea. But as it turned out, there were a lot of nice humans here.

The school I'd attended had been mostly for witches, and I'd kept my head down at college and mostly associated with those I knew. Again, mostly witches.

Now, it was kind of nice to be able to weave between the different communities, not that the humans knew what I was, of course.

I turned back to the flowers I'd been arranging when my last customer had come in. A phone order had come through for a large bunch of lilies and violets. Simple, but lovely.

I was so tempted to use my magic to make them bright, bigger, more beautiful. But there were severe consequences for revealing magic to the non-magicals.

So, instead, I practiced my hand skills. I arranged them in a nice bunch, wrapping paper and plastic around the stems, then tying it off with an orange ribbon to contrast the vivid purple color of the violets.

The bell above the door tinkled as a new customer pushed it open.

"With you in a moment," I called over my shoulder toward the front door, and a tingle of awareness shot up my spine.

I shivered, not with cold but with impending change. My breath caught in my throat as I twisted around to see who had set off such a drastic shift in the world around me.

A huge man stood in the shop, staring at me with quiet intensity.

His rugged beauty struck me like a slap to the face. Soulful, dark blue eyes. Brown hair falling to his shoulders. Features so stunning it made me want to crawl over the counter and jump into his arms.

The only thing that stopped me from doing exactly that was the fact that the person standing before me staring at me like he'd never seen a woman before, wasn't just a man. I took a deep breath through my nose and shivered at the gruff, animalistic notes.

He was so much more than just a shifter. He was a wolf. Not just any wolf, an Alpha.

I'd come across one once by accident when I was a child in the forest. The scent of an Alpha was like barely leashed power, earthy sweat and strong animal. I'd never forgotten how I'd felt that day, and now I was standing before another one. This time, in human form.

I placed my hands on the counter in front of me, digging my nails into the wood so that I didn't squeal or scream or any of those immensely embarrassing female reactions that finding your one true love was bound to bring out in even the calmest of women.

I cleared my throat with a cough and forced myself to look up at him. "Can I help you?"

He had the brightest, sharpest blue eyes. The darkest hair. And if he wasn't six feet six, I'd bite my own bum.

"You're a witch," he said, no inflection in his voice indicating it was a question.

"Shh…" I said, hushing him. "You're lucky my boss has gone to the bank."

He frowned. "She doesn't know?"

"We don't tell humans what we are. You know that." I crossed my arms over my chest and raised an eyebrow at him. "Do you go around shouting to the humans that you're an Alpha wolf shifter?"

His eyes went wide, and he stared at me with his mouth open. He looked as if I'd hit him over the head with a frying pan.

"What's wrong? Cat got your tongue?" I asked, grinning at him for long moments.

Damn, he's beautiful. So beautiful.

Though that was probably the wrong word for his appearance. His jaw was darkened with the beginnings of a new beard and the muscles bulging under the gray hoodie he wore hinted at an incredibly lethal body.

Hot… he was damn HOT.

"What are you?" he asked, almost as an accusation.

"What do you mean, what am I?" I repeated and frowned at him. He knew I was a witch. What more did he want? "I'm Ruby. Why? What's wrong?"

"How did you know that about me?" he asked. "I'm not the Alpha… not yet, anyway."

"But it's in your blood, isn't it?" I asked, second-guessing myself now. I couldn't be wrong about that, could I? The other Alpha I'd met was in wolf form.

He took a few steps forward, his intense blue gaze staying focused on me. "Yes, it is. So, answer my question. How'd you know that?"

My breath caught in my throat the closer he moved, the scent of him so familiar, like a long-forgotten memory. But how was that possible? I'd never met him before. I was sure of it.

"I…" I swallowed and dropped my arms, grabbing for the counter again as my knees threatened to buckle beneath me. "I met an Alpha wolf when I was child. He smelled the same as you."

The Alpha crept closer until he stood right in front of the counter I was leaning on for support.

I had to tilt my head up to look into his eyes, and when I did, a noise came out of my mouth that I couldn't decipher.

A moan? A prayer? A curse?

What is this?

I gripped the counter as my trembling legs finally gave way. This was going to hurt if I didn't save myself.

I muttered a spell word and conjured a chair beneath me. I fell into it, feeling as intoxicated as I assumed drunk felt.

Witches had a great resistance to alcohol, like most paranormals, so I'd never felt what being tipsy was like, let alone been fully intoxicated. But I had to assume it felt like this strange, hot, tingly feeling that pulsed through my veins, making me weak, weepy, and strangely aroused.

Damn, that's what this is! Arousal. Heat pulsated from my core, radiating through my belly and down my legs.

I forced myself to look up at him, and he was staring at me as though he were waiting for something. "Um…" My brain had gone all stupid and blank. "Did you ask me another question?"

He shook his head and growled a little, swallowing and coughing as though he suddenly couldn't speak.

What was going on?

The bell tinkled again over the front door and Andrea strolled back in.

I jumped to my feet and made my chair disappear before she saw it.

"Welcome back," I greeted her, putting on my cheeriest smile and happiest voice, though inside my head, my world was spinning.

This guy… this wolf shifter… he had to be my soul mate. The one I'd called for on Halloween last year. Didn't he? Nothing else made sense.

He was so much hotter, bigger… older than I'd imagined.

But I'd never expected a wolf shifter. *Damn.* How was my mom gonna take this news?

Andrea placed her black handbag on the counter and frowned at the Alpha wolf in front of me. "Can I help you?"

I was surprised by her non-welcoming response, especially for one of the friendliest women I'd ever met. Didn't she feel his strength, his power? How wasn't she affected by his beauty?

Then something my mother had once told me swam up into my subconscious. *Humans don't like shifters.* Wolves, especially. They could feel the danger in them, which to us, was an aphrodisiac. However, for a human, it only smelled like trouble.

And boy, am I in trouble…

The guy nodded at Andrea and pushed a piece of paper across the desk at us.

I glanced down at it. An order of lilies and violets.

"Oh, these are for you, sir!" I squawked in my nervousness to diffuse the situation. I didn't want Andrea to be angry at him. He wasn't doing anything wrong.

I twisted around, grabbed the flowers I'd just been arranging, and turned back to him in a hurry. I leaned over the counter and offered them to the huge man I was pretty certain was meant to be mine.

"Thank you," he managed to say, though he sounded garbled and his teeth were unusually pointed as he forced the words out.

Almost… wolf-like. His teeth hadn't looked like that when he'd come into the shop.

He pulled out a credit card from his wallet and I glanced down at the name before sliding it through the sensor on the side of the register monitor. I couldn't help myself.

Jackson Davis.

Oh, I liked the sound of that. But where did he live? Where was he from? Was he just passing through town or did he belong to a pack in the area?

I have to find out!

I processed his payment and handed back the plastic.

He plucked the card from my hand with his fingertips, careful not to touch me as he took it. A flush of disappointment washed over me. I ached to touch him, to see if I could feel something tangible and physical between us.

I was early in my training as a witch, but all my teachers said I had a natural affinity for scrying. Future predictions. And my instincts were always on target.

And every instinct, every vibe, every ounce of my witchy genes, was telling me that Jackson and I would be seeing *a lot* more of each other in the future.

"Thank you," he mumbled again as he backed away, though he barely opened his mouth to speak this time.

I cocked my head at him and watched as he began to retreat. What was with the talking thing? Or more precisely, the lack of talking thing?

Was he fighting the urge to shift? Did he feel the attraction between us that radiated like the sun? I wanted to know so badly what was going on inside his head.

"Oh, ah…" I tried to call out to him as he left, but he practically ran for the door, the bells clanging as he threw himself outside.

I stared at him through the window as he hopped into his truck and squealed out of his parking spot in front of the shop before I even had time to walk around the counter.

Andrea shook her head and *tsked* loudly as she opened the cash register and began unloading the change she'd gotten from the bank. "He sounded like such a nice man on the phone. I'm sorry you had to wait on him while I was out. I'm sure he scared you."

"Scared me?" I repeated, moving away from Andrea to arrange some nearby roses. Idle hands… devil's work, and all that.

"Oh, yes," Andrea said, shuddering. "Didn't he bother you? The size of him… the feel of him. Ugh." She shuddered again.

I clenched my jaw. Why didn't she understand that there was nothing wrong with him but instead, something wrong with her?

But I swallowed down my anger. It was for the good of the humans that they were afraid of the shifters. It was natural. And I shouldn't be offended.

Even though my face was flushed with heat, and rage bubbled inside me.

It's a good thing. It's a good thing. Don't get mad.

I faced the roses I was toying with so she couldn't see my red face and forced myself to continue with normal conversation. "Who were the flowers for? His wife? Did he say?"

There hadn't been a card ordered so I was left hoping someone hadn't snagged him before I could.

"His grandmother, I think," Andrea said as she went into the back to check stock and I was left staring out the window.

Was this the man I was meant to love? The one that our Halloween spell had called upon? Everything in me said yes.

But none of us three, not Tiffany, not Bella, not me, had even had a single date since that fateful night exactly twelve months ago.

But from the feel of Jackson Davis and the prickling of the hairs at the nape of my neck, I was pretty sure I'd just met my one. My only. My soulmate.

And he was a wolf shifter.

Damn. I hope the coven doesn't mind!

Download HERE

www.ingramcontent.com/pod-product-compliance
Lightning Source LLC
Chambersburg PA
CBHW060805210726
48292CB00013B/1767